SANDRA MARTON

Roman Spring

Harlequin Books

TORONTO • NEW YORK • LONDON
AMSTERDAM • PARIS • SYDNEY • HAMBURG
STOCKHOLM • ATHENS • TOKYO • MILAN
MADRID • WARSAW • BUDAPEST • AUCKLAND

ISBN 0-373-11660-8

ROMAN SPRING

Copyright © 1993 by Sandra Myles.

Dear Reader,

Studying Latin piqued my initial interest in Rome. I was fascinated that one place should have so dominated the ancient world. When I discovered two beautiful symphonic poems by Respghii, "The Pines of Rome" and "The Fountains of Rome," I found I could close my eyes and actually "see" the city of the Caesars. When I finally saw Rome for the first time, it was as if I'd been there before. Was I once a Roman aelady who stole outside the city walls to meet my centurion lover? Did he have sapphire-blue eyes, like my hero in *Roman Spring*—and like my husband?

Enjoy!

Sandra Marton

Books by Sandra Marton

HARLEQUIN PRESENTS

CHAPTER ONE

CAROLINE concentrated on a spot on the wall while Fabbiano, kneeling on the floor beside her, whisked a needle and thread through the hem of the scarlet silk dress that clung to her like a second skin.

"My best creation," he muttered to the coterie of assistants clustered anxiously around him, "and see what has happened to it!"

Their eyes shifted to her accusingly, as if the hem's collapse were her fault.

"Turn," the designer commanded, jabbing her in the leg with a pudgy hand. "Quickly, quickly, *signorina*. Now, stand still."

The needle snicked in and out of the fabric, and then he leaned back on his heels, scowling.

"Carlo. The chalk."

An assistant stepped briskly forward and slapped a stick of yellow chalk into Fabbiano's outstretched hand.

"Pins."

Another slap. Caroline's lips quivered. She had a sudden vision of the designer's rotund form draped in green surgical scrubs. Surely next someone would step up and wipe his brow.

"Scissors."

The little man's hand shot out again and Caroline quickly raised her eyes to the ceiling. Don't smile, she told herself sternly. Think of something else. Think of how surprised the well-heeled audience beyond the velvet curtain would be if it could see what was going on back here, the last-minute mayhem that came of packing a dozen models and heaven only knew how many assistants, hairdressers, make-up people, and general, all-purpose "gofers" into the cramped space that lay backstage at the *Sala dell'Arte*.

No. That was the wrong thing to think about. It only reminded her of how she and Trish had hooted with laughter when they'd seen the engraved invitations that had gone out in three languages for this evening's showing.

"'The Hall of the Arts'," Trish had read in her flat Midwestern twang. "'What locale could be better suited for the unveiling of Fabbiano's stunning Fall Collection on behalf of the Children's Aid Fund?'"

"The local *pescheria*?" Caroline had suggested with an innocent bat of her long lashes, and the roommates had dissolved in giggles.

"I agree," Trish had said when they'd stopped laughing. "The fish market would be just the right setting for Fabbiano's designs, but no one's going to say so."

"Especially when he's been cagey enough to tie the showing to a charity affair," Caroline had added with a sigh. "All he'll get is praise. I'll bet there won't be an empty seat in the house."

There wasn't. One of the models had peeked at the audience from behind the heavy velvet curtains that draped the stage and reported breathlessly that every spindly-legged gilt chair in the crowded hall was taken.

"Wait until you see who's here," she'd whispered excitedly, then reeled off a dizzying list of names that had drawn oohs and aahs.

Even Caroline, who wasn't much into such things, had recognized some of them. Usually, Fabbiano's showings drew people very much like his designs, those who were all glitz and no substance. But tonight there was a fair sprinkling of media people and others, those with money and titles, what Trish teasingly called old blood.

"*Signorina. Signorina*, are you deaf?"

Caroline looked down. Fabbiano, still on his knees, was glaring up at her, his hands on his hips. "I ask you to turn in a circle, please. You must hurry, if we are to finish. It is almost showtime."

Well, that was honest, anyway. Showtime was certainly what this was. When Caroline had signed a year's contract with International Models, it had been because she'd wanted to learn everything she could about the fashion business. A year in Milan, Italy's great fashion center, had sounded close to perfect—at least, that was how the woman who'd interviewed her at International Models had made it sound.

"You'll work with the finest talents in the business," she'd said earnestly, "you'll make oodles of money, and you'll return to the States at the top of your profession."

Caroline hadn't cared much about that last part. Modeling was only a step on the road to a career in design. But earning enough to pay for design courses at Pratt or at the Fashion Institute in New York had been more than appealing, and working with people in the business had been the clincher. She had, in her naïveté or her stupidity—she was never sure which—imagined herself standing at the elbow of a Valentino or an Armani, learning to drape soft wools, to design things that had classical beauty.

It had seemed a dream come true.

And that was the trouble, she thought wryly. It had been exactly that—a dream. Reality had turned out to be something quite different. Oh, she liked Milan. The city was a spirited blend of the old world and the new. In the same hour, you could gaze on the incredible beauty of Da Vinci's *The Last Supper* and stroll the Galleria Vittorio Emanuele, Europe's oldest, most elegant shopping mall. And always, on a clear day, you could look up and see the magnificent, snow-capped Alps.

But not one of the agency's promises had come true. Caroline modeled not for Valentino but for Fabbiano and designers like him, whose careers would last only fractionally longer than the lives of fruit flies, whose successes were dependent not on talent but on flash and dash. As for the money she'd planned on saving—how could she? The agency took half her pay before she ever saw it, some of it in commissions for her bookings, the rest to pay her share of the rent on the miserable apartment she shared with Trish and two other girls.

But worst of all was finding that she disliked fashion-show modeling. Camera work was one thing, but she felt incredibly vulnerable shimmying in a trendy, often skimpy outfit while pop music blasted and people stared. It was, she knew, a stupid way to feel. She was a model; people looked at models. They were supposed to. It was just that she couldn't help seeing beyond those stares, to the envy of the women and the coldly calculating sexual avarice of the men.

Eventually, she'd found a way to endure her moments spent on stage. The trick was to turn off the instant you stepped on the catwalk. Not to make eye contact with anyone in the audience. Not to think about the silly outfits you were wearing or the paint slathered on your face or hair that had been whipped and frothed into a lion's mane.

Instead, you held your head high and let a glazed look mask your eyes. You moved to the music in a way that the show demanded. And all the time you weren't really there, you were somewhere else entirely, and the funniest part of it was that you ended up looking like a pro, like a model who lived for these moments in the public eye.

"D'accordo!"

Caroline started, then looked down again. Fabbiano was rising creakily to his feet, all smiles now that the crisis was over. Beaming, he clasped her shoulders and pressed kisses into the air on either side of her face.

"It is done," he announced. "You, *signorina*, are superb. Almost as beautiful as the dress you are wearing. Yes?"

Caroline cleared her throat. "It's—it's quite unusual."

"Unusual?" he said, casting his entourage an amused glance over his shoulder. "It is beautiful, young woman. It is the most beautiful thing you will ever wear—until I surpass myself the next time!"

"I don't see how you could," she said pleasantly. "You've just about gone the limit now."

The little man's eyes narrowed momentarily, but then he smiled. Even if his English permitted him to understand her answer, his ego would not.

"Enjoy yourself, *signorina*," he said with a smile, and then he hurried off, his assistants trotting after him.

"Fat chance of that," Caroline said. "Well, it's the thought that counts, I guess."

"Is that what's supposed to keep me in this dress? Positive thoughts?"

Caroline whirled around. Trish was coming toward her, her pretty face twisted in a grimace. She was wearing a chartreuse dress that looked as if it had been spray-painted on.

"My God," Caroline said with a groan, "what's that?"

"A good question." Trish lifted her hair from her shoulders and turned her back. "Do me a favor, would you? See if you can zip me up."

"I can," Caroline muttered as she inched the tiny plastic teeth shut, "if you can do without breathing. There. How's that?"

"Impossible—but who am I to complain?" Trish swung around and faced her. "It is beautiful," she said coyly, "it is the most beautiful dress I will ever wear, until I surpass myself the next time."

Caroline laughed. "You heard?"

"Yeah." She stepped back, eyes narrowed, and surveyed her roommate dispassionately. "Too bad you couldn't tell him the truth—that whatever class that dress gets it owes to you."

Caroline tugged at the thin straps that held the red silk up over the generous curve of her breasts, then smoothed down the skirt as if her touch might somehow magically make it extend beyond her thighs.

"And you haven't seen what I get to put on next," she said with a shudder. "What the heck? Another hour or so, I can get back into my jeans and—"

"Not tonight, old buddy."

"What do you mean, not tonight?"

"Don't tell me you've forgotten. The cocktail party after the showing? We're expected to mingle."

Color rose in Caroline's cheeks. "I don't mingle."

"Hey! I don't, either, remember?"

"I'm sorry, Trish. I didn't mean—"

Trish sighed. "I know you didn't. Look, tonight's different. The party's for charity. For kids."

"So? We're here to show Fabbiano's misbegotten collection, that's all."

"Exactly. And he's pledged five per cent of tonight's take to the Children's Aid Fund, which means—"

"Which means the old boy's one clever manipulator."

"Which means," Trish said patiently, "that we're on the books until the party ends. We have to smile pretty as we work our way through the ballroom so that the carriage trade will want to place orders."

"And the men can try to finger the merchandise."

Trish grinned. "I've never seen one of them manage that with you yet."

"You're damned right," Caroline said sharply. "It doesn't say a word in our contracts about us having to put up with being hit on by every male who thinks he's got the price of our bodies."

"Look, I agree. Some of these guys are jerks. And some of the girls—well, some of them seem to think the men are perks of the job."

"They're one of the horrors of it."

"Uh-huh. But try telling that to Giulia. Or to Suzie. They're both seeing guys who've promised to get them into films."

"And I," Caroline said with conviction, "am seeing no one but the cabdriver who takes me home."

"Sounds good to me," Trish said with a shrug.

"*Signorine.*" The girls turned. One of Fabbiano's assistants was standing on a low stool, clapping her hands. "Ladies," she said excitedly, "*e ora di farlo*. We are about to begin."

Caroline felt a familiar knot forming in her belly. I hate this, she thought fiercely, I hate this!

"Hey. Are you okay?"

She looked at Trish, forced herself to smile. "I'm fine."

IT WAS, he thought, one hell of a place for a man to spend a Thursday evening. Not that he didn't like women. Nicolo Sabatini permitted himself a little smile. Damn, no. No one would ever accuse the Prince of Cordia of that.

The trouble was, there were too many of them packed into this room. Beautiful ones. Homely ones. Young ones. Old ones. And all of them had one thing in mind.

The Fabbiano Collection.

Nicolo shifted unhappily in the little gilt chair that had certainly not been made for a man's body. It wasn't as if he wasn't interested in what women wore, either. He liked the softness of silk, the slippery feel of it under his hands as he slowly undressed a woman in a shadowed bedroom.

But to have to sit here and pretend interest in an endless parade of painted mannequins wearing bored looks and the ridiculous fashions he'd already glimpsed in the huge sketches plastered on the wall as decorations— Nicolo shifted again. No, he thought, no, he couldn't do it, not even for *la Principessa*. He would do anything for his grandmother, his beloved *nonna*—hadn't he proved that by accompanying her here tonight, to this benefit for her favorite charity?

But to sit here, like one of the effeminate fools smirking over there or, worse still, like Antonni and Ferrante and the others he'd spotted, who boasted of the conquests they made of the long-legged girls who dreamed of jewels and furs and sold themselves so easily—to sit here, to even be in the same room with such men, made him feel filthy.

And there was no reason for it. He could step out into the anteroom, smoke a cigar, even take a walk around the block, and still be back in plenty of time to escort *la Principessa* safely through the crowd and out the door.

Nicolo leaned toward the elderly woman seated beside him. *"Nonna,"* he said softly.

La Principessa looked up. *"Si, Nico."*

"Would you mind very much if I stretched my legs?"

She smiled. "You are restless?"

"No, not at all. I just—"

"Restless, and out of your element. I should have realized." She smiled again as she touched his cheek. "A man like you prefers his women one at a time, eh?"

He grinned, white teeth flashing in his tanned face. "You know me too well," he said.

The Princess waved her fingers at him. "Go on, Nico."

"Are you sure you don't mind?"

"Of course not. I shall be fine."

"I won't go far," he said. "If you need me—"

"I won't," she said firmly. "Now, go."

He rose from the ridiculous chair and made his way carefully down the crowded row, responding politely to those who greeted him by name, noting with carefully repressed surprise that two women who gave him private little smiles were seated next to each other, friends who had no idea they had something more than friendship in common.

It was less crowded at the rear of the room and he thought of pausing there, where he could watch *la Principessa* and still draw a breath of air that was not perfumed half to death, but then he patted the slender cigar in the breast pocket of the dinner jacket that had been hand-tailored to fit his sinew-hardened body and decided that only a whiff of tobacco would fully cleanse his nostrils of the mix of scents that hung in the overheated room.

He turned toward the door—and all at once the room was plunged into darkness and a whine of hideous music exploded from the overhead speakers.

"Dio mio," he growled, and he leaned back against the wall, folded his arms across his chest, and prepared to wait out the boredom of the long moments ahead.

Lights on the ceiling blinked to life, spraying the stage with wild colors. The curtains parted, revealing a line of models wearing too much makeup, too much hair, and not enough clothing to stretch a man's imagination. One of them stepped forward, bouncing frantically to the music, and the others followed her down the catwalk. The audience applauded, and the parade was on.

Nicolo's mouth twisted as he watched the show, for that was certainly what it was, one in which the women were as much for sale as were the clothes. What was beyond him to understand was why any man in his right mind would want to buy. Nothing so readily available was worth having, not even women as beautiful as . . .

The breath caught in his throat. A woman was moving on stage, a woman wearing a red dress. No. God, no. Heat rose in his blood. To call the bit of silk that clung to her body a dress was ridiculous. His eyes skimmed over her. The dress curved over her breasts lightly, cupping them like a man's hands. It flowed over her hips the same way, and over her buttocks. He felt his fingers flexing, and he balled his hands into fists and jammed them into his pockets.

She turned, swaying to the music. Her face was perfect: high cheekbones, a straight nose and a lush mouth. Hair, streaked with the colors of the sun, tumbled down her back and over her shoulders and swung in waves as she shimmied down the catwalk. Her hips moved slowly to a beat in the music only she seemed to hear. Her expression was cool, almost impassive, and Nicolo wondered if that was how she looked when she lay beneath a man, her flesh responding to his caresses but her soul forever untouched.

His body tightened, the muscles drawing in on themselves. The heat that had bloomed in his blood became fire, traveling straight to his loins. He felt himself quicken, felt himself focusing on her, on that dress of flame...

And suddenly, she looked directly at him. Her head turned; her eyes swept across the room, then fixed on his. *Dio*, what a face! It held the beauty of a madonna—and the promise of a courtesan.

"Her name is Caroline Bishop. She is an American."

Nicolo jumped as if he'd been singed. Gianni Antonini was standing beside him, head cocked, a sly grin on his too-soft face.

"Antonini." Nicolo cleared his throat, forced his attention from the woman. "I thought I saw you in the crowd. How've you been?"

"I can introduce you, if you like." Antonini's grin widened. "I have a—what shall I call it?—a special friendship with one of her roommates."

Nicolo's expression was chill. "I am sure you have."

The other man laughed softly. "She'll be at the party, of course. All the girls will—it's where they'll make their best contacts. Would you like to meet her then?"

Nicolo swung toward him. "Why?" he said, almost pleasantly. "Do you get a cut, Antonini?"

"Nicolo, Nicolo. You try and insult me when I'm only being friendly. You know how these American girls are. So far from home..." He smiled and nodded toward the stage, where Caroline was just disappearing behind the curtains.

"This one is more interesting than most. She plays hard to get—but anything can be had for a price."

Nicolo's mouth curled with distaste. "That would make the buyer as cheap as the seller," he said flatly as he stepped away from the wall. "*Arrivederci*, Gianni."

The soft sound of the other man's laughter followed him as he stepped into the foyer. When the door swung shut after him, he breathed deeply, drawing the cool, unscented air deep into his lungs.

Damn! Why had he let Antonini get to him that way? Let the man do as he liked. It was none of his business. There'd been no need to behave like a fool. He'd been working hard lately. Too hard. Perhaps that would explain it, why he'd lost his composure with Antonini, why he'd reacted as he had to the woman.

He smiled tightly. Although a man didn't need an explanation for that kind of attraction. The reasons for it were as old and as primal as mankind itself. Still, the incident had been upsetting. It was as if he'd had a sudden glimpse of a side of himself he didn't know, a side that was dark and uncontrolled.

It was an uncomfortable realization.

After a moment, he took a cigar from his pocket, lit it with his gold Cartier lighter, and shifted it until it was clutched between his teeth. Music spilled from behind the closed doors as the moments passed. The cigar was half-finished when he shot back his cuff and looked at his watch. Good. The showing couldn't last much longer, and then he could collect *la Principessa* and leave.

He smoked the cigar down to a stub, then ground it out. The music was changing, rising in volume, approaching what had to be a climax. The show must be ending, at last.

He took a deep breath, marched to the doors, and flung them open. Yes. The audience was rising to its feet, applauding and cheering, as the models tugged a smiling Fabbiano on stage.

Nicolo shouldered his way through the crowd toward the Princess. She looked up when he reached her, her eyes glittering.

"You missed it all, Nicolo," she said. She crooked her finger at him, and he bent down until her lips were at his ear. "The clothes were terrible," she whispered. "You cannot imagine!"

He laughed. "But I can, darling."

"No," she said positively, "you cannot. Even she—what they dressed her in was so—so *orrenda* . . ."

He laughed again and followed the old woman's pointing finger. "Who?" he said. "Who did they dress in something so dreadful . . . ?"

The laughter, and the words, caught in his throat. There she was again, standing on stage with the others, that same cool, removed look on her beautiful face. The red silk dress had been exchanged for a slender column of midnight blue sequins that caught the light and spun it back in dizzying rainbows of color.

His eyes slipped over her. The gown was long, seemingly demure—but when she shifted her weight, he caught a flash of her thigh, and when she turned—God, when she turned, he could see the length of her naked spine . . .

"Nicolo, Nicolo?"

He swallowed hard and tore his eyes from the girl. "Yes, *Nonna*?"

The old woman clutched his arm and rose slowly to her feet. "That, at least, is more becoming. Still, it is not what she should wear, not with that face. Am I right?"

"I'm sure you are," he said distractedly.

"Amazing that she should be here, no?"

He shot a last, quick glance at the girl before turning back to the Princess.

"Forgive me *Nonna*. Who are you talking about?"

"Arianna," she said impatiently.

Nicolo stared at her. "Arianna?" he said slowly.

The old woman made a face. "Don't look at me that way," she said, "as if I'd suddenly become senile."

"Darling *Nonna*," he said gently, "Arianna is not here. She hasn't been in Italy for a long time. You know that."

The Princess touched her tongue to her lips. "Of course I do," she said. "I only meant that the coincidence is amazing." She nodded toward the stage, where Fabbiano was taking bows. "Don't you see? It's incredible how much she resembles Arianna."

A cold fist clamped around his heart. There was no need to ask her who she meant. He knew, instantly; his gaze went to the girl who had so intrigued him and he was only amazed he had not seen it right away.

Yes. Of course. The resemblance was there, not so much in looks but in the way she held herself, the way she looked out at the world with that little smile that dared anyone to try and touch her, he thought, remembering. There would be a greater resemblance, too, one not just of demeanor but of morals—or their lack.

"Nico?" His grandmother took his arm. "We must meet her."

"No," he said sharply. He drew a breath, forced himself to smile. "No," he said, more gently, "I don't think it wise, darling. It's late, and your doctors would want you to get your rest."

"And you know what I would say to them! Nicolo, please, it will only take a moment."

A roar went up from the crowd. The velvet curtains had dropped over the stage, and someone had thrown open the doors that separated this room from the next. Crystal chandeliers glittered brightly above a marble floor; a quartet of musicians played music—real music, Nicolo thought, incongruously, not the brain-frying stuff they'd played during the fashion show. Serving tables, set with white damask, delicate stemware, and hors d'oeuvres, beckoned.

"Nicolo?"

He looked down. His grandmother was clutching his arm, smiling at him with an almost girlish pleasure.

"We will not go near her, if you prefer. But it is so long since I went to a party," she whispered. "Please, Nico. One little glass of wine—just five minutes—and we'll leave. Yes?"

The crowd surged forward. Nicolo sighed.

"Five minutes," he said, "and not a second more. *Capisce*?"

La Principessa laughed softly. "Of course," she said, and, with sudden surprising firmness in her step, she moved toward the ballroom.

CHAPTER TWO

CAROLINE stepped back quickly as the heavy velvet curtain descended. She was always eager for her turn on the catwalk to be over but tonight she breathed an audible sigh of relief as the show ended.

Something had gone wrong. Perhaps that was overstating what had happened out there, but, for the first time in months, she'd suddenly felt at the mercy of the audience, aware of every whisper, every stare.

"Ladies, ladies! We must not keep our guests waiting."

Caroline glanced up. Fabbiano was standing off to the side, his arm raised like a parade marshal's as he directed the models off stage. His eyes met Caroline's and he gave a fussy toss of his head.

"Do you hear me, *signorina*? Hurry, please!"

The ballroom, she thought. That was where he was herding them, and it was the last place she felt like going, especially now. It had been a long time since the mental barrier between herself and the watching audience had been broken...

"Remember, please, ladies. Smile and be pleasant, make your way through the ballroom so everyone can see you."

...and it was definitely the first time she'd become aware of one person in that audience, one watching pair of eyes...

"Heads up, stomachs in, spines straight. The hair, the face, all perfect. *Capisce*?"

...and it had been disconcerting. Very. Like—like being watched, like having her privacy violated. She'd fought the sensation as long as she could and then she'd done something she'd never done before, she'd deliberately looked into the sea of faces, looked unerringly to the rear of the crowded room...

"You! Comb your hair, *per favore. Signorina*. The skirt. Over there! Is this a funeral or a party? Smile. Smile!"

...and found a man watching her, his eyes fixed to her face with blatant sexuality.

There was nothing new about that. Men had been assessing her hungrily for years, ever since she'd turned sixteen and changed from an awkward, gangly teenager to a tall, curvaceous young woman. Caroline had never grown used to it but she had learned to ignore it, even here, in Italy, where admiring a woman openly seemed almost a national pastime.

What was different was that there had been something else mixed in with the raw hunger blazing in his eyes. It was anger, she'd thought suddenly, anger as sharp and cruel as the blade of a knife, as if he'd held her responsible for the desire so clearly etched into his arrogant, handsome face...

"I asked you a question, *signorina*. Please favor me with an answer."

Caroline blinked. Fabbiano was standing in front of her, staring at her like a disapproving schoolmaster. One of the girls giggled nervously as color flooded her cheeks.

"Well," she said, "I—er—I—"

"Just nod and say yes," Trish murmured from behind.

Caroline did both. The designer's brows drew together and then he gave her a grudging smile.

"Exactly," he said. As soon as he'd turned away, Trish slipped in beside her and Caroline angled her head to the other girl's.

"What did I just agree to?" she whispered.

"The usual warning that we strain our brains and memorize the numbers of our gowns. I suppose he's afraid he won't be able to squeeze every *lira* out of the crowd unless we direct all questions to him personally."

Caroline nodded. That was fine. It might be part of her job to parade through the ballroom but she surely didn't want to have to prattle facts and figures for what she was wearing now, a skintight concoction of bugle beads and sequins that probably cost more than she'd make for the entire year.

The door to the ballroom opened. Music and laughter wafted out like an invisible cloud.

"Ready," Fabbiano said, and for just an instant Caroline felt a clutch of something that was very close to panic. What if the man was still here? What if she felt him watching her again?

She gave herself a mental shake. What, indeed? She had a job to do, and no Italian Romeo suffering the effect of an overactive libido was going to keep her from doing it. She took a deep breath, smiled coolly, and sailed forward into the ballroom.

The room was enormous. High, frescoed ceilings looked down on a marble floor worn smooth over the centuries. She caught a glimpse of crystal chandeliers and gilt-trimmed walls covered in faded damask, much like the walls at La Scala. Had the same architect who'd designed the opera house designed the Sala dell'Arte?

She wasn't going to find out tonight, Caroline thought with a little sigh. She was here to work, to wend her way among the clusters of people gathered around the groaning buffet tables, to smile like a wax mannequin and to stop when requested, to pirouette and offer the same answer to each question about her gown whether it dealt with size, color, fabric, price or availability.

"I'm sorry, I can't help you," she kept saying, as if she were chanting a mantra. "Please direct your queries about gown number eighty-two to Fabbiano."

She could say it in English and in French, in Italian, Spanish and German; she could do a passable job in Japanese. She could probably say it in her sleep. She could—

A hand reached out and caught hold of her arm. "What a terrible color," the woman said irritably. Caroline offered a noncommittal smile. "Is it available in red?"

"I'm sorry, I can't help you," Caroline answered pleasantly. "Please direct your queries about—"

"And that high neck in the front." The woman stabbed a bony forefinger just below Caroline's breasts. "Can it be lowered to here?"

"I'm sorry, I can't help you. Please—"

The woman turned away. "Honestly," she said, "these girls sound like parrots!" Her companions laughed. "What can you expect? They're paid to be pretty, not bright."

Color stained Caroline's cheeks as she moved off. She would not do this again, she thought tightly, and the agency be damned! At least you could tune out the gawkers when you did catwalk modeling, but down here, wandering through the crowd, people treated you as if you were—

"Hello, darling. How are you this evening?"

A man was blocking her path, an Englishman by the sound of his upper-class drawl. Caroline smiled politely.

"Fine, thank you. I'm wearing gown number eighty-two," she said. "If you have any questions—"

"Well, yes, I have." He grinned, showing yellowing, too large teeth.

Two other men crowded up beside him, grinning just as foolishly. "What's your name, love?" one asked.

"I'm sorry," Caroline said pleasantly, "but—"

"Come on, darling, all we're asking is your name. Surely you could tell us that."

"I could," she said sweetly. "And now, if you'll excuse me—"

The men laughed as she maneuvered past them with a fixed smile. She could see a couple of the other models standing near the buffet table, laughing as they accepted glasses of champagne from attentive gentlemen. Fabbiano would not mind if he saw the girls beginning to blend in with the guests. Orders came in just as easily that way as they did when you strolled around and worked the room as you were supposed to. Perhaps they came more easily. She had been at this long enough to know that, Caroline thought bitterly.

"Sociability sells," the head of the International Models office in Milan said at every opportunity.

But Caroline had not hired on as a saleswoman, and she'd certainly not hired on to be sociable. She'd—

An arm shot out and snaked around her wrist.

"Here we are!" an American voice said happily. "The most provocative little number in the collection. Come here, *cara*, and let me get a closer look."

Caroline's smile stiffened. The man holding her was short
and chubby. He swayed a little as he breathed fumes of wine
into her face.

"*Yessiree*, that surely is somethin', isn't it?" he said.
"Just take a look at those lines."

He was looking at her, not the gown, but Caroline pretended otherwise.

"I'm wearing gown number eighty-two," she said pleasantly. "Please direct your enquiries to—"

"By golly, you're an American, aren't you?" He chuckled. "I should have known, darlin'. Only a genuine American long-stemmed beauty could move the way you do. That
pretty blond hair, those big blue eyes—how'd you get eyes
the same color as those sequins, honey?"

Smiling, he ran a finger quickly down the curve of Caroline's hip, then danced it around until it rested lightly
against her thigh, just at the start of the slit that ran the
length of the gown. When she flinched back, his arm tightened around her.

"Come on, darlin', hold still." His eyes met hers. "Otherwise, how can I judge what I'm buyin'?"

She felt herself flush, but she forced herself to show no
other reaction.

"That's easy," she said, her tone still pleasant. "Just ask
Fabbiano about item number eighty-two. He'll give you the
details."

"Well, not all of them, darlin'." He smiled. "For instance, I'll bet he can't tell me where you'd like us to go for
supper."

"Thank you, but I'm not hungry."

"Drinks, then. I'll just bet modelin' is thirsty work."

"Thank you, but I'm not thirsty, either."

His smile didn't waver, but Caroline could see the sudden darkening of the pale eyes.

"Now, darlin', you want to be nice to old Eddie," he said
softly. "I don't think you realize who I am."

A pig, she thought fiercely, that's who you are. But she
knew how to handle pigs. You didn't run—that only made
them eager for the chase. Instead, you looked straight into

their eyes and made it clear that you had absolutely no desire to wallow in the mud with them.

"You're right," she said quietly, "I don't. And, what's more, I don't much care."

His smile diminished just a bit. "I'm a buyer, darlin', and I've got a mighty fat checkbook. I can write this here Fabbiano a nice big order—if I like the merchandise."

"Tell that to Fabbiano, not to me. I wear it, he sells it."

The man grinned. "What is it, honey? Am I bein' too subtle for you? I'm in a position to further your career if—"

"Perhaps I'm the one who's being too subtle," Caroline said coldly. "The dress is all that's for sale."

The little man squinted; the look in his eyes became furtive. "Come on, darlin'. You don't really want Fabbiano to find out that one of his little girls cost him a whoppin' big order."

Caroline's palm tingled. One good slap across that sweating face, she thought, that was all it would take to send the little SOB reeling. She was taller than he by at least four inches, and, even though he outweighed her, it was all gut and no muscle.

But the last thing she wanted to do was make a scene. This was humiliating enough without having an audience looking on.

"Listen," she said quietly, "if you just let go of me, I'll forget this ever happened."

"Forget?" His voice was creeping up the scale. Caroline looked around cautiously. A couple of faces had turned toward them, lips curled with anticipatory amusement. "Hell, darlin'," he said, "*I'm* the one who's gonna have to forget. *I'm* the one's been insulted, the one's been—"

"Is there a problem here?"

The deep male voice was cold, harsh, and touched with the faintest of Italian accents. Even though Caroline had never heard it before, she knew immediately to whom it belonged.

A little thrill of anticipation ran along her skin as she turned and looked into the eyes of the man who'd watched her with such intensity during the fashion show.

He was tall, even by her standards, and she stood five feet
ten in her stocking feet. He wore a perfectly tailored black
tuxedo, but nothing could disguise the strength or power of
the broad-shouldered body beneath the elegant clothes. His
hair was dark and curling, his skin lightly tanned. His features were almost classically Roman in their masculinity: a
straight, aristocratic nose set above a sensual mouth and
strong, squared chin.

But it was his eyes that were most compelling. They were
a blue so deep that it was almost sapphire, and were thickly
fringed with dark lashes. Promenading the catwalk, Caroline had felt their blazing heat. But it was the American who
stood beside her who felt that heat now, she thought with a
little shudder. He was on the receiving end of a look that was
as coldly disdainful as any she'd ever seen.

"Perhaps you did not understand me, *signore*," her res-
cuer said, very softly. "Is there some difficulty here?"

"No, no, there's no difficulty at all," the other man said
in a voice that was just a shade too affable. "The little lady
and I were just talkin' about where to have dinner." He
looked at Caroline and grinned. "Isn't that right, darlin'?"

The blue eyes swept to hers; that cool, glittering stare held
her transfixed.

"Is that correct, *signorina*?"

Caroline looked back at him and suddenly she thought of
an old fable, the one in which a traveler had to choose which
of two doors to open, knowing that behind one lay safety
while behind the other crouched a tawny black-and-gold tiger.

"Signorina?" The man's mouth twisted. "If you are
planning to spend the evening with this gentleman, you have
only to say so."

"I already told you she was, pal." The American became
bolder, his hand sliding up Caroline's arm. His fingers were
sweaty, his touch proprietorial, and all at once she wrenched
free and turned to the man who'd come to her assistance.

"No," she said quickly, "I've no wish to have dinner with
this—this person."

"You will if you want to keep your job," the American said sharply, all pretense at good humor gone from his voice. "We all know how this racket works and—"

"Yes. We do." The Italian's blue eyes slipped to Caroline's face again; for an instant, she saw something more deadly than disdain in their depths, and she thought again of the coiled black-and-gold power of the tiger. "Which is why the lady has already promised me the pleasure of her company tonight. Isn't that so, *signorina*?"

Her mouth dropped open. "I—I—"

"There is no need to be shy, *signorina*," he said coldly. "Business is business, after all. Surely this—gentleman— understands that a prior commitment must take precedence over his needs tonight."

Caroline flushed. He had ridden to her rescue like a knight on a white charger and now he was insulting her. Well, he could just take his insults and his offers of assistance and—

"Caroline." She spun around. Arturo Silvio, the modeling agency's Milan chieftain, was bustling across the floor toward her. He was smiling, but there was no mistaking the harsh displeasure in his eyes. "I see you caught the attention of two of our most important guests. Mr. Jefferson— how are all those stores in Texas doing? And Prince Sabatini." His smile became even more unctuous. "What a great honor to see you here tonight, sir. Is the Princess with you, perhaps?"

The Prince smiled thinly. "Why else would I be here?"

Silvio's smile never wavered. "Of course. I see you've met one of our loveliest girls. Caroline, dear—"

"Model." Caroline had spoken without thinking. All three men turned toward her. Her eyes lifted to Nicolo Sabatini's and, for a brief instant, she saw something beyond disdain shine in their deep blue depths. Amusement. Yes, she thought furiously, it was amusement! Her chin lifted in defiance. "I prefer to be referred to as a model, Signor Silvio."

"How delightful, Caroline," the agency head said through his teeth. "Charm, beauty—and spirit, as well."

"What you ought to do is teach these girls some manners," the American muttered crossly.

This time, the Prince's amusement was obvious. "Excellent advice," he said pleasantly, "especially since it comes from such a paragon of good behavior."

"Listen here, Prince—"

"Your Excellency, please—"

Sabatini held up his hand. "I am certain you gentlemen can entertain each other. As for the lady—she had already made her choice. She and I were about to have a glass of champagne." He looked at Caroline and gave her a smile that never reached his eyes. "Isn't that right, *signorina*?"

No, Caroline thought, of course it isn't right. Why would she want to go with this man? His insults had been no less cutting than the American's, they'd just been delivered with more urbanity.

"Signorina?" Sabatini offered her his arm. "Some champagne?" His polite smile did nothing to diminish the flat ultimatum in his eyes. Come with me, he was telling her, or accept the consequences.

And the consequences made her shudder. She had no wish to be left stranded with the horrible Mr. Jefferson nor with the oily Signor Silvio. As for Prince Nicolo Sabatini—his intentions were certainly not honorable. It wasn't just the way he'd looked at her; it was more complex than that. Men, especially those with money and power, often saw women as either good or bad. There wasn't much question into which category an Italian blue blood would place a long-legged American blonde living and working far from the protection of home and family.

But what did that matter? Surely only the most decadent of aristocrats would make a play for another woman while his wife was in the same room. Sabatini was only setting things up for another time. He had, apparently, seen the Texan making an unwanted play for her and he'd come to her rescue so that he could put her in his debt for a future evening.

He'd made a mistake in judgment, but that was his problem, not hers.

"Caroline." Silvio's smile strained at his teeth. "His Excellency is waiting for you, my dear."

Caroline tossed back her head, curved her lips into the same sort of bright smile she wore on the catwalk, and took Sabatini's outstretched arm.

"Thank you, Your Excellency," she said. "Champagne sounds lovely."

He smiled coolly, gave a nod in the general direction of the other two men, and set off across the ballroom with Caroline in tow. People glanced at them as they went by; the ugly little scene they'd played out had not gone unnoticed. A woman's laughter rang out and Caroline flushed and tried to quicken her step, but the man beside her would not match it.

"Slowly," he said. "There's no need to run."

"Everyone's looking at us," she hissed.

"Indeed." His voice was curt. "And what would you expect them to do, *signorina*? They have just witnessed a performance as good as the one you gave on the catwalk."

She gave him a quick, angry glance, just enough to see that his mouth was thinned with displeasure.

"If you didn't want to be part of my 'performance,'" she said sharply, "you should have kept out of it."

"Perhaps I should have. But it is too late now for regrets, and so we will take our time."

"Doesn't it bother you that people are staring?"

He laughed. "Do I look as though I care, *signorina*?"

Caroline glanced up at him again. No, damn him, he did not. He looked like a man with nothing more on his mind than reaching the bar on the far side of the room—and yet she could feel a tension in the muscle of his arm, see it in the set of his mouth.

"Besides, it is you they look at, *signorina*." He gave her a quick, chill smile. "But then, that is what you want them to do, isn't it?"

She flushed. "If you mean I want them to look at my gown, you're correct."

"The gown, yes." His mouth twisted with distaste. "And the body beneath, which you display to such obvious advantage."

They had reached the bar. Caroline took her hand carefully from his and looked at him.

"Thank you for your help, Prince," she said coldly. "But—"

"That is not how one addresses me," he said, his teeth showing in a humorless smile. "You may refer to me as 'Your Excellency.' Or 'Your Highness.' As you prefer, Caroline."

The arrogant bastard! Perhaps he expected her to curtsy. Caroline drew herself to her full height.

"And I," she said more coldly than before, "am referred to as Miss Bishop."

He made a little bow. "Of course. Forgive me for having addressed you so informally, *Miss* Bishop."

Caroline's gaze flew to his face. His smile was more genuine this time. Anger welled within her breast. Why wouldn't it be? He was laughing at her, the rat! A flurry of harsh retorts sprang to her mind, but she bit them back. She would not lower herself to the level he clearly thought suited her. She would, instead, walk away from him with her head high—and his unsavory hopes for the future dashed to the ground.

It was enough to make her manage a tight smile.

"That's quite all right, Your Highness. It would seem we've both made errors in judgment this evening. And now, if you'll excuse me—"

His hand clamped on to her wrist as she turned away. "Not so fast, Miss Bishop."

Caroline looked at him over her shoulder. "Let go of me, please," she said quietly.

"Just where do you think you are going?"

"That's none of your bus— Ouch!" She swung around and faced him, her eyes flashing dangerously. "You're hurting me!"

He stepped closer to her, close enough so she could smell the scent of an expensive masculine cologne, see a muscle knotting and unknotting in his jaw.

"I am not finished with you yet, *Miss* Bishop."

"Listen here, you. If you think—"

A man balancing two flutes of champagne jostled against him and Sabatini glared at him, then at Caroline, and his hand wrapped firmly around her wrist.

"We will not discuss this here," he said grimly.

"We will not discuss it anywhere, mister. If you think you're going to get some kind of reward for—"

"You have a short memory." His fingers were like a circle of steel around the bones of her wrist as he began moving again. Caroline had no choice but to trot alongside as he strode toward an arched doorway. "You forget how to address me—"

"I didn't forget anything," she said furiously. "Americans don't bother with such nonsense."

"—and that you are in my debt. You don't really think I risked making a fool of myself for a quick thank-you and a handshake, do you?"

"You must be joking."

He thrust her through the archway and into a small anteroom where a fire blazed in an ancient fireplace, then swung around and faced her, his eyes glittering coldly like chunks of a harsh autumn sky.

"Do I look as if I am joking, Miss Bishop?"

Caroline twisted her hand from his grasp.

"You've wasted your time, Your Highness," she said, her tone painting the title with contempt. "If you think what happened out there gives you a claim to me—"

"Would you have preferred I leave you to the tender mercies of your American admirer?"

"I would have managed," she said with more conviction than she felt.

"Yes." He smiled unpleasantly. "I am sure you would. After all, an hour with a man like that is a hazard of your profession, isn't it?"

She had no awareness of trying to strike him. She knew only that suddenly her hand was upraised, that his shot out with lightning speed and caught it in midair.

"You—you son of a bitch," she hissed, her breasts rising and falling rapidly beneath the gown, "you—you bastard. You—"

"You must learn to sheathe your claws, *gattina*. If you do not, you will have to pay the consequences."

"Really?" Enraged beyond endurance, she met his look of controlled anger with one of defiance. "What will you do if I don't? Torture me? Throw me into a dungeon at the

Castello Sforzesco? In case you'd forgotten, this isn't the Middle Ages. You can't—"

"No. I cannot." She gasped as his hand tightened on hers and drew it swiftly behind her back. The sudden motion brought her forward a step, so that all at once they were barely a breath apart. His eyes moved over her face and he smiled tightly. "But then, there are far more effective ways of reminding a woman who is master, *signorina*."

His eyes grew dark, as they had been when Caroline had first seen him from the catwalk. He shifted his weight so that his body brushed lightly against hers. She could feel the heat of him, the hardness of muscle that lay hidden beneath the elegant cut of his dinner jacket, and all at once there was a subtle shift in the atmosphere, as if the anger that burned between them could, in the flicker of a heartbeat, become something even more primitive...

"Nicolo?"

Their eyes met, and Caroline's heart began to race. He was going to kiss her, she thought wildly, he was going to bend her back over his arm and put his mouth to her throat, and she—she would close her eyes, she would arch her body to his...

"Nicolo, you have brought her to me! Ah, *che bella*. I must have fallen asleep—but then, that is the prerogative of an old woman, isn't it?"

Nicolo Sabatini blinked. He looked at Caroline like a man rising from a deep sleep, and then his face hardened. He took a rasping breath, dropped her hand and turned toward the fireplace. Caroline, heart still pounding with anger and confusion, did the same.

A woman, leaning lightly on an ebony-and-silver cane, was rising slowly from the depths of the high-backed chair that had hidden her from view. She was small, obviously frail, with silvery white hair drawn back from her face and secured in a knot at the nape of her neck. Her skin had the beautiful, paper-thin translucence of great age. But her smile was bright and her eyes—as blue as Nicolo's—glinted with happiness.

"Nico," she said, her eyes on Caroline's face, "I think perhaps you should introduce us."

Caroline watched as the Prince's face underwent a metamorphosis. A heartbeat before, he had looked at her with blind passion, then with something that bordered on contempt. Now, as he looked at the old woman, his expression became soft, almost tender.

"*Nonna.*" He smiled. "I did not mean to disturb you. Were you sleeping?"

"Resting, Nico." Her smile broadened. "It is a long time since I have had so much excitement."

"Yes." He gave Caroline a cool look, as if the old woman's admission were somehow her fault. "That is true, *Nonna.*"

The woman smiled at Caroline. "Pay no attention to my grandson, my dear," she said. "He is angry because I did not keep my promise to go home early. But how could I, without meeting you first?"

Caroline managed a bewildered smile in return. "I'm sorry," she said, "I'm afraid I don't—"

"Nico? Where are your manners? Introduce us."

"Forgive me, *Nonna.*" He gave Caroline a quick unpleasant glance. "Caroline Bishop, may I present my grandmother, *la Principessa* Anna Sabatini?" His mouth twisted. "Nothing would do but that she have the honor of meeting you, *signorina* despite my best efforts to convince her otherwise."

The Princess laughed. "Quite right, Signorina Bishop. I sent him into the ballroom, with instructions that he was not to return without you."

Caroline's head swiveled toward Nicolo Sabatini. She had been wrong, then. He had not been determined to put her in his debt because he wanted to seduce her. His intentions had been honorable, even if his behavior had left something to be desired.

A pang of conscience sent a light wash of pink into her cheeks. She still didn't like him. He was too arrogant, too proud, too ready to sit in judgment on her, but—

"Come, Miss Bishop." Princess Sabatini smiled and patted the chair nearest hers. "Sit here with me, and we shall chat for a while." Sighing, she sank into her seat. "I spent much time in the States when I was a girl. New York. Washington. Florida..."

The old woman's voice trailed off. Caroline hesitated, then took a step toward the fireplace, but Nicolo Sabatini swung toward her.

"She will want to talk forever, longer than is good for her," he said, very softly. "You will not let her."

"No. Of course not. But I don't understand why—"

"What an expressive face you have, *cara*." He smiled coolly. "Of course you don't. And it disturbs you to realize that I did not come after you for the reasons you thought, doesn't it?"

Caroline's blush deepened. "Your Excellency—"

"I am sorry to have disappointed you. It must be a rare occasion when you meet a man who does not want you in his bed."

Her face stung as if he'd slapped it, but her eyes held defiantly to his.

"Not as rare as it is for you to meet a woman who wants to be there."

"Basta!" His hands shot out and caught hold of her shoulders, and in that same instant, his grandmother's voice called his name.

"Nicolo? Are you still there? Be a good boy and get us something to drink, will you, *carino*?" The old woman peered around and smiled. "I am sure Miss Bishop and I would both like some champagne."

Caroline took a deep breath. What she wanted was to slap Nicolo Sabatini's face, to stalk out of the Sala dell'Arte and never look back.

But the Princess Sabatini was no more responsible for her egotistical grandson than she was for tonight's overblown charity event. She was merely an old woman who wanted to spend a few minutes in nostalgic memory of long-ago visits to America.

Caroline gave Nicolo a final cold glare as she wrenched free of him.

"Champagne would be lovely," she said, and she made her way to the Princess's side.

CHAPTER THREE

TRISH YAWNED as she came padding into the kitchen the next morning. She headed straight for the coffeepot.

"Mmmf," she said, wincing at the bright sunlight streaming through the window.

Caroline, who was seated at the table trying to make sense of at least the headlines in *Osservatore Milano*, looked up.

"And a cheery good morning to you, too," she said mildly.

Trish made a face as she poured herself coffee. "There is no such thing as a good morning," she grumped, burying her face in the fragrant steam rising from the cup. She took several gulping swallows before finally lifting her head. "Not until after I've had my first sip of coffee," she said. "You should know that by now."

Caroline grinned. "I do—but it doesn't keep me from hoping that some morning you'll come bouncing into the kitchen with a smile on your face—"

"And a song in my heart." Trish shuddered as she collapsed onto the chair opposite Caroline's. "Not unless you believe in miracles, I won't." She sipped at her coffee again, then put down the cup and propped her head on her hand. "Well?"

Caroline looked up from the paper again. "Well, what?"

"What do you mean, 'Well, what?' You know what I'm asking. What's happening?"

Caroline searched the other girl's face and saw the question there. A faint wash of color rose under her skin as she rose from the table and walked to the counter.

"The usual," Caroline said, deliberately choosing to misunderstand the question. "Suzie and Giulia haven't showed up yet."

"It's only 8:00 a.m." Trish made a face. "They're probably still partying. I meant, what's happening with you?"

"With me?" Caroline hesitated. "Well, I don't have anything scheduled until this afternoon, so I thought I'd try getting in to see Signor Silvio and see if I can pry my money free of his sticky grasp." She filled her cup with fresh coffee. "Honestly, how they get away with such stuff—it's bad enough they take a large commission, but to sit on the money as long as they do..."

"I didn't mean that, and you know it."

Caroline turned slowly. "I'm afraid I don't understand—"

"Come on, this is me, remember? I was at that party last night, the same as you."

"So?"

"So," Trish said patiently, "we left the Sala dell'Arte together, we bought *gelati* and gained a billion calories eating it, we came home, scrubbed the goo off our faces and plopped into our beds—and in all that time, you never said a word worth hearing."

Caroline frowned. "What does that mean?"

"You know what it means. Everyone saw that gorgeous prince carry you off—"

"Oh, come on!"

"Well, he did! He saved you from the clutches of the greasy little man by carrying you off to that back room—"

"It was an anteroom."

"—and closing the door. And—"

"It didn't even *have* a door! Dammit, Trish—"

"And you didn't come out again for an hour," the other girl said triumphantly. "And when you did, you didn't say a word about what had happened in there to anybody!"

Caroline's brows lifted. "Nobody asked," she said wryly.

"Well, I'm asking now. You can tell me. I won't breathe a word."

"All right," she said, after a moment. Her eyes met Trish's. "I had a chat with the Prince's grandmother."

The other girl stared. "You did what with who?"

Caroline grinned. "I met his grandmother, the Princess Sabatini." She took a sip of coffee. "And we talked for a while."

"Are you serious?"

"Absolutely. Want some more coffee?"

"What did you talk about?" Trish demanded, her expression a mixture of bemusement and incredulity.

"This and that. The States, what I've managed to see of Italy... Actually, I think I reminded her of someone. She kept saying I look like Adrianna. Or Arianna." Caroline shrugged her shoulders. "Whatever. It was pleasant—and it was harmless. In fact, it was fun."

"Fun," the other girl echoed.

"Yeah. She sort of reminded me of my own grandmother, back in Vermont." Caroline smiled slightly. "It was nice. Really. She's a sweet old lady."

Trish leaned back in her chair and grinned. "Well, that's a novel way to get to a man's heart. Some girls show a guy they're terrific cooks—and my roommate shows him she can make friends with his granny! Interesting approach, kid. Did it work?"

Caroline grimaced. "What do you mean, did it work? I told you, it had nothing to do with Nicolo Sabatini. Once he'd introduced me to the Princess, he never said another word." She looked at Trish across the rim of her cup. "As for finding his heart—the only way I'd want to do that is with an ice pick."

Her roommate giggled. "I take it you weren't swept off your feet by the guy."

"That's an understatement."

"Still, he was interested in you. Come on, come on, don't try and deny it. Giulia told me he was looking at you the way a starving man looks at a plate of pasta."

"An apt description if I ever heard one. Trust me, Trish. You've met the type before. He sees women as a movable feast—and himself as first in line at the table."

Trish nodded. "He made a pass, huh?"

Caroline remembered that moment when she had thought Nicolo was going to take her in his arms. She remembered the heat in his eyes, the promise...

"Right?"

Shrugging, she turned away from Trish's bright look of inquiry. "More or less."

"And you, being you, set him straight." Trish grinned. "I wish I'd been there to hear it. What'd you say? 'Prince, I'm not interested?' "

"You don't address him that way."

"What way?"

"You don't call him 'Prince.' "

"No?"

"No." The girls' eyes met. "Now that I think about it, back home Prince is either the name of a rock singer—or a dog," Caroline said slowly. "You know—'here, Prince. Stay, Prince. Sit, Prince.' "

" 'Down, Prince,' " Trish added helpfully.

They smiled, giggled, and all at once they were whooping with laughter. Caroline collapsed into a chair.

"Thank you," she gasped.

"For what?" Trish said, holding her sides.

For putting last night into perspective, Caroline thought. But she didn't say that. Instead, she smiled.

"For putting me in the right frame of mind for facing that rat Silvio. After all, asking him why my pay's late is always good for a laugh."

IT WAS ALWAYS difficult—sometimes impossible—to get an appointment with the head of the agency's Milan office, or, at least, it was like that if you were one of the agency's models. Silvio's receptionist was always terribly sorry, but *il signore* was busy.

But not today. To Caroline's surprise, the woman actually sounded pleased to hear her name.

"Signorina Bishop," she said, "I was about to call you. Signor Silvio wishes to see you."

Caroline stared at the telephone in her hand. "He does?"

"He has a job he wishes to discuss with you. Will ten o'clock be convenient?"

Caroline said that it would, then hung up. Silvio never discussed jobs, he simply assigned them. Her pulse gave a thud. She'd heard of an opening for a showroom model at one of the better fashion houses on the Via Montenapoleone; despite the agency's insistence on scouting all jobs itself, she had gone around to the house and applied for the position herself, listing International Models as representing her. Could it be...?

It was too much to hope for. Still, as she made her way up the narrow staircase to the agency office at five minutes to ten, it was hard to contain her excitement. Modeling at Adorno's would be steady work; it would pay well and, even after the agency took its cut, she'd have money left over. And the designers at Adorno's had an eye for fashion. There'd be so much to learn about fabric, about draping...

The receptionist looked up as Caroline pushed the door open.

"Ah, Signorina Bishop. You are right on time."

Caroline nodded. "Yes. Is Signor Silvio—"

"He is waiting for you." The woman leaned across her typewriter and flashed a smile so chummy it was almost a grin. "There is nothing like an excellent opportunity to make a girl prompt, eh, *signorina*?"

An excellent opportunity. Caroline's heart thudded again. She was right, then. Adorno's had telephoned the agency. They wanted her. Oh, Lord, they wanted—

One of the doors swung open and Silvio emerged, both hands held out to her, his round face beaming.

"My dear," he said. "Please, do not stand outside. Come in, come in, and sit down."

Caroline fought back the urge to glance over her shoulder and make certain he was really talking to her. She smiled hesitantly, ignored the outstretched hands, and stepped into Silvio's office. It was sparsely furnished and grimy. A smudged window overlooked an alleyway. To the right, a partially opened door led to a connecting office.

He motioned her to a chair opposite his desk.

"Would you care for some coffee? No? Tea, then." He gave a forced laugh. "I never remember which it is you American girls prefer, my dear, coffee or tea—or is it chocolate? I am certain my girl can—"

"No," Caroline said quickly, "thank you, *signore*, but I don't want anything." She swallowed. "I just—I'd like to talk about this job offer."

Silvio's smile seemed to slip a notch. "Of course. I simply thought you might wish to make yourself comfortable before we did."

"I appreciate that." She drew her breath. "But—but I'm just so delighted about it, that—"

"You know of it, then?"

"Well, yes. Sure." Caroline hesitated. "It was my idea, after all."

His eyes widened. "Yours?"

She nodded. "Yes. I know we're not supposed to solicit jobs for ourselves, but—"

Silvio laughed a shade too heartily. "No, no, that's fine." He leaned forward. "But must we use that word, solicit? Such a nasty word, don't you think? As for worrying about my displeasure..." He spread his hands. "If our girls are enterprising enough to find unique positions for themselves, who are we to object?"

She nodded again, all thought of her overdue money forgotten in her excitement. "I hoped you'd see it that way, *signore*. When do I start?"

Grinning, he tilted his chair back on its legs and folded his hands across his ample paunch.

"I must say, Signorina Bishop, your—enthusiasm—surprises me. You are not known for having such a cooperative spirit."

"I think I've been very cooperative," Caroline said quickly. "No designer has ever complained about me."

"Well, not the designers, no." He gave an expressive shrug. "But some of the clients..."

Last night. That damned buyer with honey on his voice and whoring in his heart... Caroline shifted in her chair.

"If you're referring to what happened at the Sala dell'Arte," she said, "I'm sorry. I never intended to make a scene, but—"

"You need not explain, *signorina*." Silvio's chair hit the floor with a thud as he leaned forward again. "It has all worked out for the best, yes? The gentleman was most pleased. He has made an excellent offer to us, and—"

Caroline blinked. "I thought it was a woman who ran the House of Adorno."

"Adorno? What has Adorno to do with this arrangement?"

"Why—why that's the job, the one I went after." She stared at his blank face. "Isn't that what we're discussing?"

Silvio threw a quick glance at the connecting door. "We are discussing the offer made us this morning by His Highness, the Prince. He has agreed to—"

Caroline felt the blood drain from her face. "The Prince? Do you mean—Nicolo Sabatini?"

"Exactly. He had agreed to pay us more than our usual commission—well, I explained, of course, that we would need ample compensation to lend him one of our girls for such unusual services, and I must say—"

"Services?" Caroline leaped to her feet. "Services? Are you insane?" She slammed her hands on the desk and papers flew in every direction. "I don't perform 'services'!"

"*Signorina*, please. You must calm yourself." Silvio looked at the door again. "I only meant—"

"I know exactly what you meant, you pig!" Her voice shook with rage. "You and that—that slimy Prince, that—that—that—"

"Slimy?"

Caroline spun toward the connecting door. Nicolo Sabatini, dressed in a navy pinstriped suit, white shirt and crimson silk tie, smiled at her.

"I am disappointed, Miss Bishop. I have seen enough American films to have expected something more colorful than that."

"Yeah? Well, stick around, Prince," she said, her tone making it clear that her deliberate misuse of the title was meant to insult him. "Give me a minute and I'll come up with something that will turn your face the same color as your tie!"

Silvio rose to his feet. "Your Highness—"

"Get out, Silvio."

"Excellency, I was just about to explain the details of your proposition to the *signorina*—"

"With all the subtlety at your command, no doubt." Nicolo jerked his head toward the door that led out to the reception area. "You've done enough," he said sharply. "Now, get out!"

Silvio's chair scraped as he shoved it back. He rounded the desk quickly, made an apologetic bow of his head to Nicolo, frowned at Caroline, and scurried to the door. It opened, then swung shut.

Nicolo blew out his breath. "So much for leaving things to those who are the least capable," he said. He walked slowly toward the desk. "Please, Miss Bishop, won't you be seated?"

"No." Caroline tossed her head. "There's no point. If you think your—your wonderful offer is going to sound any better coming from you than from that—that pig—"

"He is not a pig at all."

"No? Well, I suppose not, considering your part in this sleazy little scheme. But—"

"He is another animal entirely." Nicolo scowled, leaned back against the desk, and crossed his arms over his chest. "The man is an ass."

"I'm telling you, he's—he's . . ." She stared at him. "An ass?"

"Exactly so. And you, Miss Bishop, are a fool."

Caroline's brows lifted. "I beg your pardon?"

"Didn't I make myself clear last night? Then let me do so this morning. I am not interested in buying your services."

"Oh, please! I've just sat through the most incredible proposition, and now you expect me to believe—"

"A business proposition. I do not buy my women," Nicolo said coldly.

"No?" Her smile was thin. "What *do* you do, then? Shower them with expensive gifts to keep the lie alive? Is that what Silvio was going to explain to me next, that you'd agreed to pay the agency a commission but that you were going to give me—what? Jewels? A diamond ring? A fur coat? After you'd enjoyed my services, of course."

A cool smile curved across his lips. "I see you put a high value on yourself, Miss Bishop."

Caroline's head came up. "Believe me," she said quietly, "you could never afford me, Your Highness."

The smile came again, quicker and somehow more knowing than last time.

"I would not have to," he said softly.

"Listen here—"

"Because, if I wanted you, you would come to my bed eagerly, *carina*."

"That's it," she said, flushing with anger. She turned away. "Don't think it hasn't been interesting."

He stepped away from the desk and moved toward her. His hands closed on her shoulders.

"Let me go," she said.

"Why do you deny it?" A muscle moved in his cheek. "What is between us is—"

She twisted angrily against his grasp. "Is intense dislike!"

Nicolo laughed softly. "I agree." His hands slid up her throat and cupped her face. "But what has that to do with desire?"

"My God, how you flatter yourself! I don't desire you, Prince Sabatini. In fact—"

His fingers brushed lightly across her lips, tracing a path of flame that she felt even in the midst of her anger.

"I have heard that you play this game," he said softly.

"It's not a game, damn you! If you don't stop this—"

"On the contrary. And it is most effective. It gives a man the feeling that you must be won." He smiled as his thumbs skimmed lightly across her cheekbones. "Or taken. It cannot be a simple illusion for you to maintain, when you know you've given yourself many times before."

Caroline caught his wrists. "You bastard! What gives you the right to talk to me this way? Is it because I've hurt that insufferable ego of yours? Was I supposed to fall in a heap when the great Prince Nicolo Sabatini made a pass at me?"

A deep furrow appeared between his dark brows. "You delude yourself, Caroline. I made no pass."

"Liar!"

His nostrils flared. "I don't lie. Ever."

"Well, you're lying now."

His hands fell away from her. "If you were a man," he said furiously, "I would—"

"Yes. That's the trouble, isn't it?" She showed her teeth in a taunting smile. "I'm not a man, and you can't deal with the fact that I'm just not interested."

"The only reason I so much as spoke to you last night," he said through his teeth, "was because of my grandmother."

"Really? Well, where's your grandmother today? Or are you going to tell me you made Silvio this—this proposition on her behalf, too?"

"Yes. I did." His voice changed; she could hear the sudden edge to it, the tone of imperious command. "*La Principessa* wants to see you."

"My God, that's pathetic! You're hiding behind an old woman who's not here to defend herself!"

"It is, unfortunately, the truth. I would prefer it otherwise, but she has asked for you."

Caroline shrugged her shoulders. "Well, that's nice. But I'm afraid you'll have to tell her that the days when Rome ruled the world are over. I'm busy."

Nicolo's nostrils flared with distaste. "I am sure that you are. But her wish is important to me. I have promised to bring you to her."

"How unfortunate for you." She turned and started for the door. "Look, tell her that you tried, okay? Tell her you did your best, but—"

"She is ill."

The words were delivered with a flatness that stopped her with her hand on the door.

"Ill?" she said slowly, as she turned toward him.

"Yes."

There was only the one word, but something in the way he looked made her hesitate.

"She was fine last night."

Nicolo laughed hollowly. "How fine can a woman be at *La Principessa*'s age?" He thrust his hands into his pants pockets, stalked to the grimy window, and peered out into the alley. "It is as much my fault as hers. I should not have let her attend that ridiculous affair, but she insisted."

Caroline touched the tip of her tongue to her lips. "She's probably just overtired."

He sighed. "That is what I hope. A day or two of rest, some clear broth . . ." He turned and looked at her. "And a visit from you, Caroline. It would do much for her, I think."

Caroline stared at him. Was he telling her the truth? Was his grandmother really ill, or was this only a ploy?

No matter what undercurrents had passed between them last night, it had been true enough that it was *la Principessa* who'd sent her grandson to collect her at the Sala dell'Arte. And even she had to admit that what she'd seen the Prince show the old woman had seemed to be genuine respect and affection—

"It is as Silvio, that fool, told you. But not as he made it sound. I will pay the agency's usual commission for your services, plus a bonus for any inconvenience this causes them in their scheduling. And I will pay you your regular hourly fee plus fifty per cent. If you think there is a more equitable arrangement to be made, you have only to say so."

"All this, if I'll agree to visit your grandmother."

He nodded. "Yes."

"I can see why Silvio was so happy. It's a generous offer."

"Certainly it is." A smile twisted across his lips. "You do not often spend your time with the elderly, do you?"

Caroline felt her cheeks flame. Damn the man! He was doing it again, saying one thing but making it sound like quite another. But then, he was a man used to buying whatever he wanted, a man used to having his own way.

"Well? Are we in agreement?"

"No." The word slipped from her lips. "No," she said more forcefully, "we are not. I'm afraid I'm not for sale, Your Highness. I'm sorry your grandmother's not feeling well, but it has nothing to do with me."

His eyes went dark. "I see."

"Give her my best, please, but explain that I'm very busy, that I can't possibly—"

"Oh, I know what to tell her," Nicolo said sharply. "It's what I should have told her last night, when she sent me after you." He strode toward her, his shoulder brushing hard against hers as he headed for the door. "I shall explain that you've no time in your life for such nonsense. What is an old woman's heart when compared to the joys of dancing half naked down a catwalk while the world watches?"

"That's insane. I don't dance half..." Caroline swung around and looked after him. "What do you mean, her heart? What's wrong with her heart?"

"Nothing, except that you have somehow touched it. But then, I have never subscribed to the myth that wisdom accompanies old age." His hand closed around the doorknob. "Good morning, Miss Bishop."

"Wait." She took a deep breath. "Did she really ask for me?"

A look of distaste fluttered across Nicolo's face. "Why else would I be here?"

She hesitated. "I did like your grandmother. She was very sweet and kind, and..." Caroline took another breath. "All right. I'll go see her."

She saw the look of surprise on Sabatini's face but then, he couldn't have been any more surprised than she was. She had certainly not planned on saying that, it was just that there was no reason to hate an old woman just because you hated her insufferable grandson, especially when she reminded you, in some indefinable way, of your own grandmother—but why should she explain any of that to this man? She could see that he was at a loss for words—which was reason enough for her to be pleased with her impetuous decision.

He nodded, then shifted from one foot to the other. "Well." He cleared his throat. "I suppose I should say thank you."

"And graciously, I'm sure," Caroline said dryly. "But you needn't bother." She smiled tightly. "I'm not doing it for you, I'm doing it for your grandmother. Besides, I don't want anything from you, Your Highness. Not a thing."

Nicolo stiffened. "I could not have said it better myself," he said coldly. "Now, let me get Silvio in here with a contract—"

"You misunderstood me," she said sharply. "You can sign whatever papers you like with the agency. You're quite right, they will lose money on me today." Her eyes met his. "But I won't take a penny from you for visiting the Princess."

Nicolo's eyes narrowed. "I'm afraid I'm not following you."

"It's really quite simple. I don't want to be paid for going with you to see your grandmother. It's a visit, not a business deal. Do you understand?"

He stared at her while the seconds flew past, and then he shook his head.

"No," he said flatly, "I do not."

Caroline smiled slightly. "I didn't think you would. But that's the deal, Your Highness. Take it or leave it."

He frowned, and his gaze moved slowly over her face. Finally, he shrugged his shoulders.

"Very well. If that is how you wish it—"

"It's the only way."

Nicolo nodded and pulled the door open. Silvio, crouched just outside, all but tumbled into the room.

"Oh," she said sweetly, "be careful, *signore*. I wouldn't want you to hurt yourself."

Silvio nodded nervously, his eyes darting like black ants from her to Nicolo.

"*Grazie, signorina*. I appreciate your concern."

"The lady is quite right, Silvio." Nicolo smiled tightly. "If you're going to get your neck broken, I want the pleasure of doing it."

"*Signore*, please—"

"Come on, man, get moving! Where's the contract? And where do I sign it?"

The agency chief almost groaned with happiness. "Right there, sir," he said, whipping a document from the desk. He beamed at Nicolo. "The *signorina* is going with you, then?"

Nicolo's eyes met Caroline's. "Yes," he said shortly, "she is."

Scowling, he scanned the page, then scrawled his name at the bottom.

"*Signorina?*" Silvio said, pushing the paper toward her. Nicolo's scowl deepened.

"She is not signing it," he said.

"Not ... ? But—"

Nicolo brushed past Silvio and clasped Caroline's arm. "Let's get going," he said brusquely.

She nodded. "Absolutely. The sooner I've seen your grandmother, the sooner I can say goodbye to you for the last time. And what a relief that will be!"

She had meant to put him in his place. He looked down at her, at her outthrust chin and flashing eyes, and, to her surprise, he laughed, really laughed, in a way he had not done before.

"Do you always speak your mind, *signorina?*"

"Yes," she said. "Always."

His eyes darkened just a little. "It is an interesting quality in a woman," he said, "one I have not encountered before."

"Well then," she said as she swept past him out the door, "you're in for a bumpy ride."

"Yes," he said, and he laughed again in that same, easy way.

For the very first time, Caroline wondered if she had let her instincts mislead her. But by then Nicolo was hurrying her down the steps, out of the building, and into a black Mercedes limousine.

It was too late to wonder about anything.

CHAPTER FOUR

A MERCEDES. Of course, Caroline thought as she settled inside the car. It would have to be something like this, an expensive limousine with a uniformed chauffeur and darkly tinted glass that guaranteed privacy. What other sort of automobile would a man like Nicolo Sabatini have?

The only trouble was that intelligent people didn't willingly take a car into the heart of a city as busy as Milan on a weekday. Like every other city she could think of, this one was a mass of snarled traffic. Cars moved sluggishly while pedestrians, and, of course, Italy's omnipresent, *motos*, scooted past them.

But the man beside her would no more have walked or ridden a motorcycle than he would have willingly been parted from this—this blatant symbol of money. Although, she thought, as she glanced at him, in truth she'd expected something other than this staid automobile. She could more easily picture him in a Maserati. No. In a Ferrari. To her eye, Ferraris were masterpieces of elegantly understated design, with fine lines and an innate animal grace. They were cars that spoke of power and masculinity—like Prince Sabatini himself.

Caroline shifted uneasily. What a ridiculous thing to think about a man she detested. But then, perhaps it wasn't. She had an eye for the clean lines of a good design, didn't she? Admitting that he was easy on the eyes was simple artistic honesty. It certainly didn't change the fact that she disliked him intensely.

She glanced over at him, seated cross-legged beside her, watching as he tapped an impatient tattoo with his fingers against his thigh. They had joined a Gordian knot of vans, taxis, and automobiles that was inching forward at a pace that had set that little muscle in his jaw to knotting and unknotting.

It was no more than he deserved. Every now and then, a man like this one needed a reminder that he could not control everything in this world, despite all his money and his terribly blue blood.

What was even more satisfying was knowing that she had given him that same lesson, not once but twice, this morning when she'd stunned him by agreeing to see his grandmother on her own time, and last night, when she'd turned away his advances, and never mind all that pretense about his not being interested.

Of course he'd been interested. Men always were, especially men like this one. She'd have been like the Mercedes, another symbol of his wealth and authority.

A smile came to her face. She wondered how much Nicolo Sabatini would value her if he saw her as she preferred to be, wearing faded jeans, a cotton turtleneck pullover, and grungy running shoes, her hair loose and straight or, at the most, drawn back in a French braid. If she looked like that, he'd probably have walked right past her. He'd—

"Stupido!"

Caroline looked over at Nicolo. He'd given up trying to drum his fingers into his thigh. Instead, he was leaning forward, peering through the glass that separated them from the chauffeur and glaring furiously at the car in front of them.

"There was an opening," he said, "but the fool ahead of us did not move quickly enough."

Caroline gave him a cool look. "How unfortunate."

Nicolo muttered under his breath, leaned forward, and slammed the privacy panel shut.

"It is better not to watch these imbeciles drive," he said through his teeth.

"And better still not to be one of them. You should have known the streets would be impossible."

"Thank you." It was her turn to be on the receiving end of that angry glare. "If there is one thing I definitely need at this moment, it is a commentary on Italian traffic from a girl from the American Midwest."

Caroline's brows lifted in puzzlement. "Why would you think that?"

"Only one born to the insanity of Italian traffic should make observations about it," he answered tersely.

"I meant, why would you think I'm from that part of America?" She looked at him. "For that matter, how would you even know about the Midwest?"

"I am not ignorant of your country, *signorina*. I have been there many times, both for business and for pleasure."

"I'm sure you have. To New York. To San Francisco." Caroline had to smile. "But to the Midwest?"

"One does not have to visit that section of America to know that it is famous for women with your look."

"Really." She shifted sideways in the seat and looked at him again. "And what look is that, Your Highness?"

"That look," he said impatiently, slashing his hand in her general direction. "Tall. Blond-haired. Blue-eyed. That look of farm-girl innocence." He threw her a sharp glance. "I am sure it earns you a great deal of money."

There was an undertone to the words that set Caroline's teeth on edge. She swung away from him and stared out the side window.

"You're very sure of everything," she said coldly. "And very wrong. I'm from New England, not the Midwest. And you don't need to be Italian to know that insisting on bringing a car in this mess isn't very bright. If you'd put aside that—that conceited arrogance of yours, you'd have figured that out and taken public transportation. I know that would have meant mingling with the masses, but—"

Her outburst only made him laugh. "You accuse me of being conceited and arrogant? You should listen to yourself, Caroline, and then you would know how readily—and foolishly—you make assumptions."

"I'm simply pointing out that there were better ways to have made this trip today."

"I think not."

The simple statement was delivered with such smug certainty that it made Caroline's blood heat. But she clamped her lips together and didn't rise to the bait. He had done a good enough job of getting her to do that already, and she'd be damned if she was going to give him the satisfaction of letting it happen again. She could manage that. All she had to do was keep reminding herself that she wouldn't have to bear his company much longer. Soon, she'd be sitting opposite *la Principessa*. And, as far as she was concerned, the sooner the—

Caroline swayed as the car made a sudden move. Her body brushed against Nicolo's. The contact was quick, no more than an instant, but it was unnerving. It was like—like being brushed with fire.

She pulled away and scrambled back to her side of the seat, but not before he gave her a knowing little smile. The man was beneath contempt, she thought, and she gave him her most innocent smile in return.

"So, what are you the prince of, anyway? Italy? Europe?" Her smile grew even sweeter. "The world?"

As she'd expected, that smug look of his gave way to a scowl.

"Nothing so grand, *signorina*. I am only the Prince of Cordia."

"Cordia. Cordia..." She sighed. "Can't say that I've heard of it."

"No. You would not have, unless you were a student of history. Cordia was a principality that vanished more than two hundred years ago."

"Fascinating," Caroline said, in a tone that made it clear the topic was anything but. "It must be interesting, owning a useless title in this day and age."

Nicolo's scowl darkened. "One does not 'own' a title. It is a responsibility passed on through the generations."

"And what a responsibility," she said, running her hand over the glove leather seat of the Mercedes. "What an awful burden to—"

The car made another sharp maneuver and she fell against him again. This time, the hint of flame was even stronger.

"Must your driver go so fast?" she demanded.

Nicolo shrugged. "He is trying to make up time."

"For what? We can't have very far to go now. And we're not entered in a road rally."

He sighed. "Sit back and relax, Caroline. It will make our hours together easier."

"Only a miracle could manage that!" She folded her hands tightly in her lap and stared straight ahead. "Where is your apartment, anyway?"

"I do not have an apartment in Milano."

"Your house, then. I don't care what you call it. All I want to know is why it's taking us so long to get there!"

"I am not Milanese," he said, his tone implying that such a thing should have been obvious, even to an American.

"No?"

"No. I am Roman. I brought *la Principessa* to Milano only so she could attend last night's showing. The Children's Aid Fund is her favorite charity."

"Yes, she told me." Caroline frowned as she glanced out the window. Traffic had lessened and the Mercedes was picking up speed, but the streets were unfamiliar. "What hotel is she at? It seems we've passed—"

"Why would she be at a hotel?"

"Look, have I missed something? If your grandmother's not waiting for us at a hotel, then where—"

"She is waiting for us at home." He gave her a cool smile just as the car gave a throaty growl and leaped forward. "In Roma."

Caroline's mouth went dry. "In Rome?"

"Of course."

"But—that's hundreds of miles from here!"

He gave a negligent shrug. "We will fly it in less than—"

"Fly? You mean, we're going to the airport?"

"Certainly. It would take hours to drive the distance."

Caroline swung around and faced him. "Wait a minute! Wait just a damned minute—"

"You will not use vulgarity in my presence," he said, giving her a look of absolute coldness. "Such language may be suitable in the world you inhabit. But in mine—and in my grandmother's—a woman knows what it means to be a lady."

A sound burst from Caroline's throat. "You—you pompous, egotistical, obnoxious..." She drew a ragged breath. "How dare you make speeches to me about what's proper and what's not? You—you lied to me, damn you! You—you told me your grandmother was—"

She gasped as Nicolo reached out and caught her by the shoulders.

"Watch what you say to me, *signorina*." His voice was rough with barely suppressed fury. "A Sabatini is not a liar."

"No? Then what was that ridiculous story about your grandmother being ill and asking for me? How could you use an old woman to—"

"I have used no one! I am bringing you to *la Principessa*." His nostrils flared with distaste. "Although why I let her talk me into doing such a foolish thing is beyond my comprehension."

"Is it?" Caroline demanded. "Or did it suit your plans, after that miserable failure last night?"

"Failure? Failure of what?"

"Come on, let's not play games! You tried to seduce me, but it didn't work. So now—"

"And you accuse *me* of having an oversize ego? *Per Dio*, listen to yourself!" Nicolo's hands tightened on her shoulders. "For the last time, I did not try and seduce you."

"You did. And I'm damned if I'm going to permit you to—"

"Is this what it means to be a liberated woman? To curse? To besmirch a man's honor?" His eyes flashed a warning. "To accuse him of failure because your own ego cannot survive the knowledge that a man does not want you?"

"That is so ridiculous! It's—It's—"

"If I had tried to seduce you," he growled, "you would know it."

Caroline's eyebrows lifted. "Meaning, I suppose, that I'd have fallen over in a swoon?"

A tight smile curled across his mouth. "Meaning," he said slowly, "that you would have spent the night in my bed."

"You're unbelievable! Impossible! You—"

"You would have spent the night in my arms, Caroline," he caught her hands in one of his as she began to raise them, "crying out my name as I touched you, begging me to take

ou over and over again, until finally the sun chased away
he darkness.''

She was twisting in his arms, hating the soft, insolent tone
of his voice, the smug little smile on his mouth, hating, too,
he fact that she felt powerless. She was not a petite girl, she
never had been; she was strong and healthy from years of
watching her diet and hard, sweaty workouts in the gym.
She prided herself on her strength—and yet this man, who
had already proven he could stand up to her verbally, was
holding her off as if she were a feather.

"You—you insufferable bastard!" she panted. "Do you
always get what you want?"

He laughed. "Always," he said, and his mouth dropped
o hers.

His kiss was a complete surprise. Whatever else he might
be, instinct told her Nicolo Sabatini was not a man to force
himself on a woman.

What was he proving, then? That he could overpower
her? He had already done that; what greater proof did he
want than her immobility in his arms? That he was impossible to resist? But she had resisted him. She had!

Her heart missed a beat. What was he doing? His mouth,
so hard and demanding at first, was softening, moving
slowly over hers.

Did he think she could be won over with gentleness? Did
he think—did he think . . . ?

His teeth closed lightly on her bottom lip. She gave a little whimper, and instantly the tip of his tongue stroked
gently across her flesh. A sound, the barest whisper of
something that might have been a moan, rose in her throat.

Something was stirring deep inside her. Heat. Heat, rising and spreading through her blood like the morning fog in
a Vermont meadow, like—like—

"Caroline." Nicolo whispered her name against her
mouth, and, without knowing she was doing it, she whispered his name in return, parting her lips, opening them to
his. His tongue slid against hers; she shuddered, not with
anger nor with displeasure but with some dark, deep emo-
ion.

He murmured in Italian, words she could not understand, let go of her wrists, and swept her into his arms,
gathering her to him until her heart was pressed tightly to
his, until her hands lifted and slipped around his neck. His
kiss deepened. It was the kiss of a man who wanted a
woman, who knew she wanted him. It held passion and fire,
it was a kiss of domination that asked for surrender yet
promised surrender in return.

When he put her from him, she made a soft sound of
distress.

"Caroline."

Her eyes blinked open—and her face flamed scarlet.

He was watching her with eyes that blazed, not with passion but with cold satisfaction.

"You see how it is, *cara*," he said calmly. "If I had
wished to have you, I would have done so." He smiled easily and ran his knuckles lightly down her cheek. "That you
spent the night without the pleasure of my company was my
decision, not yours."

Caroline's reaction was instantaneous.

"You—you—" Her hand shot up and Nicolo caught hold
of it and twisted it down into her lap.

"Perhaps it is time we discussed the rules that will gov-
ern the unfortunate time we spend together until I return
you to Milano tomorrow."

"You'll return me to Milan immediately, do you hear?
I've no intention of—"

"Tomorrow," he repeated sharply, "after you have seen
la Principessa, after you have sat with her and given her
pleasure. Is that understood?"

"Who do you think you are?"

"You have asked me that before, and I have told you."
His lips curled with amusement. "Although now, I think,
it would be best if you called me 'Nicolo,' yes? Besides, my
grandmother will expect a lessening of formality, while you
are in my home."

"I am not going to Rome! You'd better get that through
your thick skull! And you'd better let go of my wrist. Dammit..."

"You have already forgotten the first rule. I told you, there will be no more vulgarity. Perhaps the other men you know find it stimulating to hear such words come from the face of a woman who has the beauty of a madonna, but I do not." His eyes held hers. "And you will do all you can to make my grandmother think you are happy to see her again."

"I would be, if it didn't mean I had to see you, as well!" Caroline slammed her free hand into his chest and he caught it easily, imprisoning it, as well. "Do you have any idea how much I dislike you?"

"If it cheers you any, be assured that the depth of feeling you hold for me is more than returned in kind."

"I don't understand you," she said furiously. "If you hate me so, why are you so insistent on dragging me to Rome? Is it really so important to you to get your own way?"

"I told you, I do this for *la Principessa*. For her sake, you will smile and pretend to be the sweet, charming young woman she so foolishly believes you to be." A harsh smile angled across his mouth. "I am not asking so much of you, after all. You are an excellent actress, *cara*. I have seen you on stage, pretending to sensuality, when in truth you are frigid as a winter storm." His smile twisted. "Or is it that you play the Ice Queen only to capture a man's interest?"

Caroline twisted her hands free of his. "You'll never know," she said, staring back at him as she rubbed her wrists. "Because as far as I'm concerned, if I never see you again..."

"Yes. That is fine with me. Tomorrow, I will return you to Milan, and, if we are fortunate, neither of us will ever have to see the other again. But first, you will do what you can to please a tired old woman. Do we understand each other?"

Caroline glared at him. "Do I have a choice?"

He smiled coolly. "I see that we do, indeed, understand each other."

"It's just that I doubt that your grandmother sent you after me with instructions to—to abduct me and drag me to Rome at any cost."

He shot her a quick look. "You will not say that to her."

I'll say what I damned well please, Caroline thought. But then she remembered the white-haired, fragile old woman she'd met last night, and she sighed.

"No. I won't." She gave him an angry glare. "But not out of any consideration for you."

"Yes." He leaned forward and threw open the privacy panel. They were obviously nearing the airport; signs announcing the different terminals were flashing by. "I must admit, your ready acquiescence surprised me. I was prepared to tell *la Principessa* you could not pay her a visit."

"Yes. I'm sure you were. In fact, I'm sure you were prepared to tell her I didn't care if she was ill or not."

Nicolo shrugged. "I just said—"

"That I surprised you." She blew out her breath. "Well, you haven't surprised me, not one bit. You're exactly the way I thought you'd be."

His laughter was quick and easy. "I take it that is not meant as a compliment."

"You take it right," she said stiffly. There was a silence, and then she looked at him. "You haven't said how long the trip will take."

He shrugged. "What you really want to know is how long you will have to play at being a lady. Not to worry, Caroline. You will be home before lunchtime tomorrow."

She thought of the shoot lined up for tomorrow morning at Paolo's, a relatively new design house, and shook her head.

"I must be home tonight," she said positively. "I've an engagement with—"

"That is impossible."

"Nothing's impossible," she said tightly. "Haven't you spent most of the morning proving that?"

"Nonetheless, returning you to Milano before tomorrow would be."

"You make me sound like a package," Caroline said angrily as she swung to face him. "Returning me to Milan, indeed! I am perfectly capable of getting home on my own, thank you." She turned away, folded her hands tightly in her lap, and stared out the window. "Surely there's a return flight this evening?"

Nicolo frowned. "I took you from Milano. I will return you to it."

"That's remarkably noble," she said with great sarcasm. "But I must be back tonight. I told you, I've an engagement with Paolo. And I can't afford to miss it."

"*Dio Mio*! Have you no shame?" He threw her a glowering look. "I have no desire to hear the details of this assignation, I assure you."

Caroline's mouth dropped open. "What assignation?"

"And if you are afraid this man will know of me, that he may learn you have spent the night with me—"

"I am certainly not spending the night with you!"

"A figure of speech," Nicolo said tautly. "The point I make is that you need not worry. Your lover need not know of our little trip."

"Listen here! Paolo isn't my lover. I'm talking about a business engagement—"

"I told you, I have no interest in the details, Caroline." His voice was sharp and cold as ice as he plucked the cellular handset from its receptacle and held it out to her. "Call this Paolo. Tell him there has been a change of plan, that you cannot be with him tonight."

Caroline glared at him. "I know why your grandmother is ill," she said. "It's because she had to deal with you, day after day."

"Very amusing. Nonetheless, it is your choice. Call him, or stand him down, as you prefer."

"It's stand him up, not stand him down. If you're going to use American idioms when you're handing out orders, at least get them right." She grimaced. "Anyway, I can't phone him. I don't know his number."

"Ask the operator." Nicolo smiled coldly. "I'm sure it will surprise you to hear that Italy is a civilized country. We have such things as directory assistance."

"Directory assistance can't help me," she said, ignoring the taunt. "I don't know Paolo's address."

"All you need is his last name."

It was, she knew, the moment to clarify things, to explain that Paolo was a company, not a man.

But the chance to make Nicolo Sabatini look like a fool was too good to pass up.

"Actually," she said sweetly, "I've no idea what his last name is."

Nicolo turned and stared at her. "I see," he said frostily. "You have an engagement—"

"An appointment. Yes. And—"

"With a man. And yet, you do not even know his full name." He said something in Italian and even if Caroline didn't understand the words, the meaning was clear enough.

"No," she said. She lifted her hand and examined her fingernails with care. "I'm afraid I don't. I didn't make this appointment myself, you see. Silvio took care of it for me."

"Silvio. He makes such—arrangements—on your behalf?"

She shrugged and lay her head back on the seat. "Sure. I suppose I could manage on my own, but—"

"And you are not embarrassed to speak of this?"

"Why should I be? A job's a job. Besides, I came to Italy to work. Why would I want to do anything that would lessen my chances of making money?"

"And yet," he said after a moment, in a voice that was almost a whisper, "and yet, last night, when you thought I was interested in you . . ." He drew a breath. "You made it quite clear you were not interested in me."

"Absolutely. I've always reserved the right to choose who I spend my time with."

"And I am not such a man."

Caroline looked straight at him. "No," she said, with a polite smile, "you certainly are not."

He said nothing, did nothing, and for a few seconds, she thought she had finally silenced him. Then all at once he grabbed the phone and barked an order into it. The car swung to the right and pulled onto the verge, and he swung towards Caroline, his eyes blazing with such anger that she had to keep from cringing into the corner.

"Listen carefully, *signorina*," he growled, "because I have no intention of saying any of this again. I am taking you to my home, into the very bosom of my family. If it were not for my concern for my grandmother, I would—I would put you out of the car right now, I would let you wait beside the road until someone took pity on you and offered to drive you back to Milano." He drew a deep breath into his lungs. "But I have given my word to *la Principessa*, I have said I would ask you to come with me, and you have agreed. God only knows why, but you have. And so, as long as you are under my protection—"

"I am here because I choose to be," she said sharply, despite the rapid race of her pulse. "I can take care of myself. I think we'll get along much better, once you've gotten that through your head. As for being under your protection..." She tossed her head. "If this is what it's like to be under your protection, I'd bloody well like to know what would happen if I weren't!"

For a moment, Nicolo simply looked at her. Then he gave her a smile so chill, so filled with cunning, that it drove the blood from her face.

"Disobey me," he said, very softly, "and perhaps you will find out."

He leaned forward and pounded his fist on the driver's compartment. Instantly, the car leaped back onto the roadway. It took long moments before Caroline calmed down enough to remember that she had not sprung the little trap she'd set. Nicolo Sabatini still thought she was a woman who supplemented her income through occasional dalliances with men willing to pay for the pleasure of her company.

She gave him a quick glance from under her lashes. His face was set and hard; except for the muscle knotting in his jaw, he looked as if he'd been sculpted of stone.

Setting him up so he'd look foolish had been ridiculous. What was the point? After today—correction, she thought grimly, after tonight—she'd never see him again anyway. Besides, they were pulling to a stop, outside a chain-link fence. Ahead, a small jet waited like a sleek silver bird beside the runway.

Caroline's mouth tightened. Let the bastard think whatever he liked.

CHAPTER FIVE

THE JET was sleek, even more luxurious than the limousine—and it belonged to Nicolo. "Sabatini," it said, in discreet gold script on the fuselage, above a representation of a lion and a shield. Inside, the same logo appeared again, on the leather headrest of the deep seats, on the breast pocket of the cabin attendant, even on the coffee service that was brought out within minutes of their being airborne.

Caroline declined the coffee but accepted a magazine. Not that she read it; it was just easier to bury her face in its glossy pages than to have to endure Nicolo's stony-faced silence. The trip was mercifully brief, little more than an hour, and soon they were standing on the tarmac at Ciampino Airport.

"Now what?" she asked stiffly.

Nicolo's hand closed impersonally on her elbow. "Now," he said, "we drive."

She had to almost trot to keep up with his long-legged, impatient stride, which was a novelty considering that usually she had to slow her pace to accommodate others, even men. Slow down, she thought, as her high heels beat a hurried tattoo against the pavement, but she didn't say it. No matter what the situation, she would not ask Nicolo for mercy. Besides, how far away could his limousine be? Surely there'd be one here, too, a twin to the Mercedes in Milan.

His pace slackened when they entered a lot filled with cars. He led her down a row, then came to a halt.

"What's the matter?" she said. "Did your driver forget to meet you where he was supposed to?"

Nicolo scowled as he dug a key ring from his pocket.

"Your tongue is sharp, Caroline." He gave her a little push in the small of her back toward a lean black Ferrari.

"Go on, get in. The sooner I get you to my grandmother's side, the sooner this ends."

Caroline blinked. A Ferrari? Yes, she thought as she folded her long legs into the car. A Ferrari, just as she'd imagined.

All right, she thought as the car roared to life. So he wasn't chauffeured about in his native city. So what? And it was interesting that his car was the one she'd envisaged, but what did that mean? She glanced over at his harsh profile. Only that he had more money than he could count, but she knew that already.

She sank back in her seat. It was a tough life Nicolo Sabatini led. No wonder he couldn't understand anyone who worked for a living. A man like this would not rise at dawn, hurry off to work, and return home hours later, weary and exhausted.

Well, tomorrow he'd get a taste of reality. A self-satisfied smile curled over her lips. He had promised to return her to Milan in the morning. She could just see his face when she told him *her* mornings began at six. The great Prince Sabatini would not relish starting his day at such an hour.

Prince Sabatini. Caroline lifted her hand to her mouth and tapped her index finger lightly against her lips. How she hated calling him that, not just because she had an American's disdain for such outdated nonsense but because Nicolo obviously relished his title. Why else would he use it?

Well, he would not hear it from her again. He'd suggested she use his first name and she would, even if there was an unwelcome hint of intimacy in it. Anything was better than having to choke out another "Your Highness."

Nicolo, she thought, tasting the name on her tongue. Much as she hated to admit it, it was a nice name, masculine, strong, yet soft and pleasant to the ear. But "soft" wasn't the word to describe the man himself. Caroline threw him a quick glance. No, certainly not. The finely tailored clothing he wore did nothing to hide the granitelike hardness of the body beneath. If anything, it enhanced it, made you aware of the broadness of his shoulders, the firmness of his muscles, the long, lean power of his legs...

"I can almost hear your brain working, Caroline."

Color raced along her skin. She looked at him. He was intent on the road, but there was a cool smile playing across his mouth.

"You are figuring how many minutes and hours you will have to endure in my company."

She let out her breath. "Oh, I've already done that," she said with cool nonchalance. "And it's far too many." For the first time, she turned her attention to the road. A sign flashed by. "Via Appia Nuovo." She felt a little surge of disappointment. "This is a highway," she said, almost to herself.

Nicolo glanced at her. "Indeed," he said dryly. "What did you expect?"

Caroline flushed. "I only meant..." She shook her head. "Nothing."

"A dirt path? A ditch?" He glanced at her again, his expression even cooler than before. "Why do Americans always think theirs is the only country that's part of the modern world?"

She swung toward him. "What I expected," she snapped, "was that Italians might show some reverence for the past. But I'm sure it was much more important to pave over history and build this—this *autostrada* than to worry about preserving something like the Appian Way!"

"The Appian Way? But this is not—"

"No. Not anymore, it isn't!"

Nicolo looked at her. "What do you know of such things as the Via Appia?"

"Much more than you'd imagine," she said in frigid tones, "despite my being an American. And female. And a model."

"I only meant—"

"I know what you meant," she said angrily. "You're all the same. You think, just because a woman is attractive—"

He laughed softly. "But you are not attractive, Caroline." His eyes met hers. "You are beautiful."

She flushed. "The point I'm trying to make is—"

"That I am guilty of making wholesale judgments about women such as you. Yes?"

Caroline nodded. "Yes."

A smile lifted the corner of his mouth. "Ah, *carina*, but you are equally guilty."

"I am not!"

His smile widened. "'You are all the same,'" he said, imitating not her voice but its angry cadence. "'You think, just because a woman is attractive—'"

"It's not the same thing at all! Men like you..."

Her words drifted away. Men like you never give women like me a chance to prove we're real, she thought. But what did it matter? Nicolo Sabatini could think what he liked; after today, she'd never see him again.

"Yes?" he prompted.

Caroline shook her head. "Nothing." She swung around and stared straight ahead. "How long will it take us to get to Rome, anyway?"

"To the real Rome?" He laughed softly as he turned off the *autostrada*. "We are almost there. Just be patient and look around you."

She didn't want to give him the satisfaction. But the road they were on now was different; it was much narrower, lined on both sides with cypresses and pines. Nicolo slowed the car; now she could see that they were passing monuments made of stone and marble.

Ruins, she thought, with a flicker of excitement. Those were ruins, standing for heaven knew how many centuries beside this road—this road of ancient paving stones...

This was the Appian Way!

"*Sì*," Nicolo said quietly.

Caroline turned to him, at first unaware she'd spoken aloud.

"But—the sign, on the other road..."

He nodded. "A newer Via Appia, yes. But we Italians were not foolish enough to bury our past completely." He looked at her. "Would you like to stop for a moment?"

She wanted to say no, to go on treating him and everything that surrounded him with the same nonchalant air she'd managed thus far. But how could she, when what she longed to do was feel the timeless beauty of this place?

"All right," she said, as casually as she could manage.

He pulled to the side of the road and she swung her door open and stepped out. It was very quiet; except for the sigh of the wind, they might have been alone on the planet. Ahead rose a cylindrical stone-and-brick ruin faced with sculptured columns.

"What is that?" Caroline asked softly.

"The tomb of Cecilia Metella, a Roman noblewoman." Nicolo walked forward, with Caroline at his side. "She was buried here in the first century B.C."

"But why here, outside the walls of the city? Had she done something wrong?"

He smiled. "No one could be buried inside Rome in the ancient times, Caroline. It was—how would you say it?—for reasons of public health. That is why many of the most beautiful ruins along the Via Appia Antica are tombs."

"You mean, like the catacombs?"

"*Sì*. But there are other sorts of ruins along the *via*, as well." He paused. "There is a place just off the road that is especially lovely, and very, very old. Would you like to see it?"

She didn't hesitate this time. "Yes," she said, "please."

They got back into the car and drove slowly along the rutted, narrow turnoff, until finally Nicolo pointed to a low rise.

"There it is," he said softly.

He shut off the engine and silence enfolded them. Ahead, a handful of broken Ionic columns rose against the pale blue sky. Other columns lay scattered on the grass, and yet there was still such perfect grace and beauty to the place that Caroline felt her throat constrict.

"Would you like to go closer?" She nodded, and Nicolo stepped from the car and helped her out. "We are on ancient ground," he said softly, "a sacred place. This was a temple to Diana, the goddess of—"

"The moon."

"Yes. That's right. She was in love with—"

"Endymion. She came down from Olympus and made love to him while he slept. And she wove a spell over him, so that he slept forever and never grew old."

A little smile angled across his mouth. "How did you know that?"

Caroline flushed. "Why wouldn't I know it? Just because you have these—these stereotyped ideas about—"

"I only meant that not many people know anything about the old gods these days."

"Oh." She hesitated. "Well, I—I've heard some of the myths."

"Backstage, at the House of Fabbiano?"

She started to bristle, but then she looked at him and saw that his smile was open and good-humored. A little of the stiffness eased from her spine.

"No, not quite," she said, giving him a little smile in return. "My grandmother had a passion for legends and fables. She used to tuck me in at night and tell me the most wonderful stories."

"Ah. She lived with you, then?"

"She raised me. That's why..."

Caroline fell silent. That's why I agreed to visit *la Principessa*, she'd almost said, but what business was that of his? Her private life had nothing to do with him.

The wind sighed again as it swept through the ruined temple, and a little shudder went through Caroline. Suddenly, she wished she'd never agreed to come to Rome, she wished—

"Are you cold?"

She started. "Cold?"

"Yes. You are shivering." Nicolo swept his arm around her. "Here, let me shield you from the wind."

"It's not necessary," she said quickly.

"I have no wish to return you to *Milano* with pneumonia. Silvio would bill me for everything from handkerchiefs for your nose to aspirin for your fever." He smiled, to show her he was joking, and turned her toward the sun. "Now, look. There's the basilica of San Sebastiano just ahead." He shifted her so she stood in front of him; his hands settled on her shoulders and he drew her back, so his body braced hers. "And the Tempio di Romolo—the tomb of Romulus—there, do you see?" She could hear the pleasure in his voice. "This is my favorite part of Roma, from here all the way to the

Porta Appia—the old city gate. If you close your eyes, you can imagine the city as it was centuries ago..."

At first Caroline listened, entranced, as Nicolo made Ancient Rome come alive. But it grew hard to concentrate. She was increasingly aware of the way he was holding her. His embrace was only an accommodation. Still, the longer she stood there, with the hardness and warmth of his body against hers, with his breath on her ear, the less she heard of what he was saying. Catacombs, churches, ancient ruins—all of it began blurring together.

It wasn't as if she weren't paying attention. She was. She was paying desperate attention. She had to, in order not to notice the faint scent of his cologne, the feel of wool against her cheek when she turned to follow his pointing finger, the deep timbre of his voice as he spoke of the Rome he loved, spoke of it tenderly, as he would of a woman...

Caroline's heart gave a dangerous lurch. She twisted free of the hands holding her and stepped away.

"Do you think we could cut this short and get going?"

Nicolo's eyes went flat. "My apologies. I did not mean to bore you. You had only to say you wished to go back to the car—"

"What I wish," she said, "is to get this visit to wherever we're going over with as quickly as possible."

"You have my word," he said coldly. "I shall get you in and out of my *palazzo* as quickly as possible."

"Your *palazzo*?" she repeated as he slammed the car door after her.

"*Il Palazzo* Sabatini." He gave her a grim smile as he pulled onto the road again. "Were you hoping to find that I am one of those fools who holds tightly to a title with no meaning? Then I must disappoint you, Caroline. The Sabatini name is very old. And very respected."

With a little sigh, she sat back and closed her eyes. "Well," she said, "let's hope it can survive the scandal of my visit."

THE PALACE was exquisite. It rose three storeys high from the cobble-stoned street, its pale stone exterior clear and uncluttered. The arched door, bearing the same lion and shield as Nicolo's plane, opened onto an enclosed atrium. Caroline caught a quick glimpse of marble floors stretching ahead to what seemed infinity, but it was the ceiling that stole her breath away. She tipped her head back and stared at the tumbling nymphs and satyrs that danced across it, trailing garlands of flowers.

"Well?"

She tore her eyes from the magnificent frescoes and looked at Nicolo. He had moved past her and stood at the foot of a soaring staircase, hands on his hips. He was a study in displeasure.

"If you want to get this visit over with, *signorina*," he said sharply, "then I had best take you to my grandmother at once."

Caroline squared her shoulders. "Of course."

She followed him to the third floor, then along the gallery to a closed door. Nicolo knocked, then pushed it open, and they stepped into a brightly lit sitting room.

"Signora Brascia?"

"Sì Eccellenza." A round-faced woman dressed in white hurried toward them. She began speaking in rapid Italian, and Nicolo held up his hand.

"In English, please, *signora*." He nodded toward Caroline. "The *signorina* does not speak our language."

"I said that *la Principessa* is quite comfortable, Excellency. Her blood pressure is good—"

"Oh, for pity's sake!" The voice from the adjoining bedroom was fragile but it carried clearly. "Emma, stop issuing medical bulletins! I am fine. Just fine! Nicolo, is that you, *caro*? Have you brought her? Caroline? Come and let me see your lovely face."

The Princess lay propped against the pillows on a canopied bed. She was smiling, holding out her hands to Caroline. Her silvery hair was held by a ribbon of the same blue shade as her bed jacket, and there was pink in her cheeks.

She's all right, Caroline thought happily. But when she got closer, she could see that the old woman's color was feverish and the hands held out in welcome were trembling.

"Ah," Princess Sabatini said with a little laugh, "you have come."

Caroline smiled as she clasped the old woman's hands.

"Of course. I was happy to have the opportunity to see you again, Principessa Sabatini."

The old woman made a face. "Such a mouthful, isn't it? Please. Call me Anna."

"Oh, but—"

"It would give me great pleasure, my dear child."

Caroline's smile broadened. "It would give me great pleasure, too."

The Princess looked at Nicolo, who had crossed the room and stood beside Caroline.

"Well, what do you say now, Nico?" she said, lifting her chin. "You insisted Arianna would be too busy to visit, but here she is. You see how wrong you are about her, hmm?"

"*Nonna,*" he said gently, "this is not Arianna. It's Caroline."

"Well, of course it is." She laughed. "A slip of the tongue, that's all." She patted the bed beside her. "Sit down, dear, and visit."

"You mustn't tire yourself, *Nonna*. Remember what the doctor said."

"The doctor! Bah! An hour with this lovely girl will do more good than all that old fool's pills! Go on, Nico. Do something useful instead of fussing over me. We'll be fine. Won't we, Arianna?"

"*Nonna—*"

Caroline looked at Nicolo and shook her head. "It's all right," she said softly.

After a moment's hesitation, he nodded. "Very well. I will have a room prepared for you. When you are ready, ring the service bell and one of the maids will show you to it."

The Princess fairly beamed. "Oh, my dear! You've agreed to stay on?"

"Well, yes. Until—"

"Hush. We will not talk of your leaving. Not just yet." She patted the bed again. "Come. Sit beside me, and tell me everything. Have you been to New York recently? What is it like? Is the Schubert Theatre still there? I can remember when . . ."

AN HOUR LATER, the Princess fell into a restful sleep, still holding tightly to Caroline's hand. Caroline freed it carefully, rose from the bed, and sank down in the chair beside it. The afternoon shadows lengthened, and she closed her eyes wearily.

So many years had passed since she'd sat with her own grandmother in just this sort of quiet companionship. She'd always felt contentment then, just as she did now. It was so lovely here. Everything was peaceful—everything but the man who'd brought her to this place.

Nicolo Sabatini was impossible. She'd met arrogant men before, but never one quite like him. So insolent. So demanding. So—so...

She stirred uneasily. So incredibly male. So virile. So capable of making a kiss into something far more intimate and passionate than a simple meeting of mouths and bodies...

"Caroline?"

Her eyes flew open as a hand dropped lightly on her shoulder.

"Nicolo!" She straightened. "I—I didn't hear you come in."

How long had he been standing there? She wished she could read his eyes, but dark shadows striped the room and masked his face.

"Come."

"But your grandmother—"

"It's all right. She's sleeping soundly."

She followed him from the room, along the gallery and down the stairs to the library, where Nicolo turned to her abruptly.

"Why did you stay with her?" he said. "The nurse tells me she's been asleep for some time."

"I know. But it seemed important to her that I be there." She hesitated. "I didn't disturb her, if that's what you're concerned about."

He watched her another moment, then turned and strode to a cabinet on the opposite wall.

"Will you have some sherry? Or would you prefer something stronger?"

Caroline hesitated, but what harm could there be in accepting a glass of wine?

"Sherry would be nice, thank you."

She strolled around the perimeter of the room as he poured the pale amber liquid, her fingers skimming over a small marble figure of a fawn, then across a tiny enameled box, and finally she paused before an oil painting of a man. The figure glowed with light.

"I see you've met Great-great-grandfather Sabatini." She turned to Nicolo, who smiled and held a glass out to her, one that seemed to have caught the rays of the dying sun. He smiled. "Actually, he's my grandfather too many times removed to count."

Caroline turned back to the painting. "I should think so. This looks to have been painted a long time ago."

"In 1560, according to family records."

"1560," she said softly. "How wonderful to have something passed down through the generations. It must be priceless to you."

He smiled wryly. "Indeed. The portrait was done by Titian."

Her eyes widened. "Titian?" She bent closer to the painting and gazed at the master's signature. "No wonder it's so magnificent."

"But you would have admired it anyway, even with no signature, hmm? Because it is old?"

"Of course. There's something special about things that come to us over the centuries." She swung toward him. He was watching her with a strange look on his face, half amusement, half something else, and she felt herself bristle. "That probably sounds simpleminded to you, considering that you live surrounded by such things, but—"

"No, not at all. It's just that I'm surprised to hear you make such an admission—"

"Considering that I'm American?"

His brows lifted. "Considering that you are a woman of this century," he said mildly. "We are a throwaway society, Caroline. It is one of the hallmarks of our time."

"Perhaps. But that doesn't mean everyone's like that."
She smiled coolly at him. "Measuring people—using worn-out clichés to categorize them—is a dangerous habit."

"Perhaps it is a habit we share, this business of vaulting to easy conclusions."

"Jumping." She couldn't help smiling. "You jump to conclusions."

He smiled back at her. "I still have some problems with the idioms," he said. "They are difficult." They stood looking at each other, and then he cleared his throat. "So. What did you and my grandmother talk about?"

Caroline shrugged her shoulders. "This and that. She wanted to know what's new in New York City—"

"And you told her."

"As best I could. I'm not an expert—I've only lived there for a couple of years."

"Ah. And you went to New York to seek your fortune, yes?"

She stiffened. "Not everyone is born rich. I moved there because I had to find a way to support myself."

"And you did."

Caroline's eyes flew to his. He was still smiling politely, but there was a hint of disdain in his tone.

"We were talking about your grandmother," she said coldly.

Nicolo exhaled sharply. "Yes. So we were. I am pleased that your visit seems to have done her so much good."

"Why does she call me Arianna?"

She could see his back stiffen. "I suppose because she is old and gets confused from time to time."

"I didn't mean that, exactly. I meant—who is Arianna?"

There was a silence before he answered.

"Arianna was—is—a distant cousin. She lived here, in the *palazzo*, after her parents died."

"She's a child, then?"

He gave a short, bitter laugh. "She was a child when she came to us. But she grew up. Oh yes, she grew up, into a beautiful, spoiled young woman."

"And?" Caroline said, after a moment.

Nicolo shrugged. "And she left us."

Us, he'd said. Us. But that wasn't the truth, Caroline thought. Arianna had left him.

"But—but why?"

"Who knows? She seemed content, at first, but then, as time passed..." He grimaced. "She craved a different sort of life. Excitement. Independence. She found life under this roof too restrictive. I had certain rules, certain expectations..."

Caroline's breath caught. He'd been in love with Arianna, you could hear it in his voice. And Arianna had been in love with him, or at least, she'd thought she was, until he'd begun taking over her life.

It was easy enough to imagine how it had gone. The girl hadn't been born into this archaic world; she hadn't been prepared for a lover who was demanding and possessive, as Nicolo must have been. What modern woman would? He'd have wished to own her, body and soul, to possess her. He'd have expected her to wait hungrily for his kisses and his caresses, to come to life when he whispered her name...

"Caroline?"

She swung around, startled, her eyes wide and unseeing. Nicolo was standing so close, so close...

The empty glass fell from her hand and shattered on the floor.

"Oh!" She knelt quickly and began scooping up the shards. "I'm sorry!"

"It's not important." He bent, clasped her wrist, and drew her up beside him. "Caroline—"

She twisted free of his hand. "You said you'd have a room prepared for me, Nicolo. I—I'm tired. I'd like to go there now, and rest."

"I want to talk to you first, about leaving here tomorrow."

"Yes." Why was she so breathless? She took a step back. "You're right, we need to discuss that. I should have told you, we have to leave very early, so that—"

"So that you can keep your liaison with Paolo?" Nicolo said silkily.

"Paolo?" She stared at him, confused for the moment, and then she remembered. "Paolo," she repeated. "Yes. I wouldn't miss that—that liaison for the world. That's why we have to leave at six o'clock sharp, and—"

"No."

"What do you mean, no?"

His smile was as pleasant as his tone. "We are not leaving at six."

"Oh, but we are!" She flung her hands on her hips. "My appointment with Paolo is—"

"Is for a photo shoot."

She stared at him. "How—how did you—"

His lips turned up in a self-satisfied smile. "Silvio told me," he said. He strolled to the sideboard, refilled his glass, and poured sherry into a fresh glass for her.

"When? This morning?" Her mouth tightened. "You mean, you knew all along, but you let me make a fool of myself?"

Nicolo turned and held out the glass. "I spoke with Silvio less than an hour ago, Caroline."

"He phoned? Well, I hope you explained that I'll be in Milan in plenty of time for the shoot, because—"

"I told him you would not be returning to Milano for a few days."

Caroline gaped at him. "What do you mean, not returning?" She strode toward him. "I agreed to stay until the morning. Hell, I didn't actually agree to anything. You forced the issue. You—"

"I was wrong."

Her mouth dropped open. Was this an apology?

"What I should have done," he said smoothly, as he pressed the glass into her hand, "was tell you that you would not be returning to Milano at all."

CHAPTER SIX

NICOLO'S WORDS seemed to hang in the silence that suddenly enveloped the room. Caroline stared at him, waiting for him to smile, to give some hint that he'd made a joke she'd simply not understood, but he only went on looking at her, his face as cool and composed as if he'd done nothing more than offer to top up her sherry.

Her mouth thinned. So much for the niceties, then. In a way, it was a relief. She'd *known* what sort of man he was from the start. He'd been more clever than the rest, luring her with an ill grandmother rather than with promises of extravagance, but now the truth was out. His talk about not wanting her had been nonsense, stuff handed out by a man salvaging a bruised ego.

Carefully, holding her temper under tight control, Caroline walked to a small parquet table and put down her glass.

"Please give your grandmother my regrets." Her voice was strong and steady; it gave no hint of her anger. "Tell her—tell her I'm sorry, but I had to leave suddenly, that I was called away..." She looked at him, at that still cool expression, and her control faltered. "Tell her any damned thing you like," she said on a rising note, "except for the truth. She's far too nice a woman to—"

"Where do you think you're going, Caroline?"

"Back to Milan," she snapped as she stalked to the door. "At least there, I know what I'm dealing with!"

"Caroline. You are being ridiculous!"

"*Arrivederci*, Your Highness. As I said in Silvio's office, don't think it hasn't been interesting, because—"

"*Idiota!*" Footsteps pounded after her. She reached for the door and started to pull it open, but Nicolo's hand closed around her forearm. He spun her toward him, slammed the door shut, and thrust his face into hers. "Must you always be such a little fool?"

"Open that door!"

"I will. When it suits me."

"Open it, or so help me, I'll—"

"I tell you, you are behaving foolishly. Your imagination is working overtime."

Caroline glared at him. "That's a laugh! You're the one with the busy imagination! How you could even imagine that I'd—that I'd ever—?"

He smiled when she began to sputter, showing even white teeth against his tanned skin.

"Yes?" He let go of her, leaned back against the door, and folded his arms over his chest. "Don't tell me you've run out of words, *cara*. I'd be disappointed."

"What I've run out of are words that would describe a man like you without—without blistering the paint on these walls!" Her jaw tightened. "And don't call me that. I am not your—your dear, or whatever that silly word means."

Nicolo sighed. "You are going to feel very foolish when this little scene has run its course, Caroline."

"Oh, no, I won't! If you think there's anything you can say that will change my mind about—about—"

"You *are* at a loss for words." He smiled. "In that case, let me help you."

"You can help me by stepping away from that door!"

"What is it you think I have offered you, *cara*? The chance to spend the night with me?" His smile grew more angular. "Why would I have brought you all this distance for one night's pleasure, hmm? Attractive as you are, Caroline, there are hotels in Milano that would have served my purpose—if a night with you had been what I wanted."

Caroline's smile was fierce and chill. "But you want me for more than one night."

He nodded.

"You want me to be with you indefinitely."

"True."

"What have I missed? That I'll have my own rooms? A car at my disposal? A charge card?"

Nicolo frowned. "I had not thought of the card," he said. "Although now that you mention it, I can see where it would prove useful. You might need to make some purchases to augment your own wardrobe."

Caroline tossed her head. "I hate to hurt you, Nicolo, but none of this is terribly original. Every one of your pals—"

"My what?"

"Oh, come on, you don't really think you're the first man who's issued me this kind of invitation?" She batted her lashes. "'Be mine, *cara*,'" she said, cruelly adopting a Continental accent, "'and I will satisfy your every wish'."

"Well," he said with a modest smile, "I will try."

"You're wasting your time. I'd sooner sleep with a snake!"

He laughed. "Caroline, really. Don't you think you should wait to hear my offer before you make such a judgment?"

"I told you, I'm not interested! Try another agency. Try another girl. Try—"

She gasped as he reached out and clasped her shoulders. *"Basta,"* he said, and all at once his smile was gone. "Enough of this foolishness, Caroline. I have no wish to make you my lover."

"Sure. And cats have wings."

Nicolo frowned. "I have an offer to make you. A serious offer."

"Lucky me!" Caroline glared at him. "You want to make me your mistress! Well, it will never happen! Never! This trip was a waste of time and effort. You showed me all your rich man's toys—the cars, the plane, the palace—and none of them impressed me." She tossed the hair back from her face. "Read my lips, Nicolo. I—do—not—want—to—sleep—with—you. Do you understand?"

"That is good news," he said coldly. "Because what I am asking you to do is become a paid companion to *la Principessa*."

Caroline's mouth fell open. "What?"

"You do remember *la Principessa*, do you not?" He gave her a smile even colder than his voice. "Or has your self-absorption swept the reason you came here from your mind?"

A flush swept into her cheeks. "Would you mind telling me what in blazes you're talking about?"

Nicolo's hands dropped from her shoulders. "I shall, now that you are ready to listen to reason." He paused for a moment, as if to gather his thoughts. "Your visit to my grandmother seems to have been most beneficial."

"So you said."

"It is what she needs," he said impatiently. "Some conversation, a little laughter..." He scowled. "And I wish her to have it. So I am asking you to stay on in Rome until her recovery is complete."

Caroline stared at him in disbelief. "You're—you're serious, aren't you?"

He stalked away from her to a cherrywood desk in the far corner. "Absolutely," he said, flinging himself down into a chair behind it.

"But..." She shook her head as she moved slowly toward him. "But I'm not a nurse."

"She has a nurse. She has the best medical care." He drew a breath, then puffed it out. "What she needs is not contained in a prescription bottle. I told you, I saw how much your visit did for her. You—remind her of someone."

"Arianna." Caroline nodded. "I know. And—I wish I could help her. But becoming her companion is out of the question."

"Why?"

"Why?" She stared at him. "What do you mean, why? Hasn't it occurred to you I've a life of my own to lead?"

"My grandmother is ill," he snapped.

"I know. And I'm sorry. But—"

"But you would sooner return to *la dolce vita* than stay here and help her get well," he said coldly.

"That doesn't really deserve an answer," she said angrily. "But I'll give you one, only because of how much I respect your grandmother. What I must return to is my job."

"Your job!"

He made a dismissive gesture that infuriated her. She slapped her palms against his desk as she bent toward him.

"That's right. My job. My responsibilities. Are you so trapped in a time of royalty and titles that you can't envisage a world in which a woman has obligations?"

His mouth twisted. "A world in which you must beg for your money, you mean. That was why you went to see Silvio, wasn't it? To get him to pay you what the agency owes you?"

She drew back. "How would you know that?"

He shrugged as he shoved back his chair and got to his feet.

"I was there for some time before you arrived, Caroline. I heard the receptionist fielding phone calls, all of them from girls demanding their pay." His scowl deepened. "Why do you go on working for such a firm?"

Caroline sighed. "I've no choice. I'm on contract to them. And anyway, I need to support myself. I have to work, or—"

"Or is it a man you hurry back to? Not Paolo, but someone else?"

The look on his face, and the sudden change in topic, caught her short. He was accusing her of having the morals of an alleycat again, and she was tired of it.

Last night, even earlier today, it wouldn't have mattered. Who was Nicolo Sabatini, anyway? Another self-centered, self-serving leftover from another age, that was who. She had been content to stand by and watch him dig his own hole with a shovel. Now, more than anything, she wanted to point him toward that hole and push.

It was time to rub that handsome Roman nose of his in the dirt.

Caroline drew herself up. "I know this is going to come as a grave disappointment," she said icily, "but there's no man waiting for me in Milan."

There was the slightest flicker of light deep within his sapphire eyes, but when he spoke, his voice was as chill as hers.

"Isn't there?"

"No. There isn't."

"Perhaps, then, that is your reason for hurrying back to Milano." A harsh smile came and went on his mouth. "To search out the next candidate, I mean. If you are between lovers—''

"Can't you understand?" Caroline flung her arms wide. "I haven't a man in my life because I don't *want* one. My life is quite busy enough, thank you."

He gave her a tight smile. "I see."

"I doubt it. You're like every other man I've ever met, you assume a woman who looks like me can't feel complete without a man, but, as a much wiser woman than I once said, a woman needs a man about as much as a fish needs a bicycle."

"What about in bed, Caroline?" His voice had gone very soft. "Would you like me to believe you have no need of a man there, either?"

Color bloomed in her cheeks. "That's none of your business!"

He shrugged. It was a deceptively lazy movement, considering the way he was looking at her.

"Or do you, perhaps, get your pleasure at a distance, by putting your sexuality on display and then treating a man who reacts to it as if he were a leper?"

Caroline's color heightened. "That's what you think, is it?" She thrust out her hand and pointed a finger at him. "Well, let me tell you something, Prince Sabatini! Any man who's fool enough to believe that a model's doing anything but her job on the catwalk—" His laughter stopped her in midsentence. "What's so funny?" she demanded.

"Silvio was right. You don't enjoy modeling very much."

It was Caroline's turn to laugh. "That's the understatement of the year."

"Then why do you do it?"

"I already told you why. It's to pay the bills—but then, you wouldn't know anything about that, would you?"

Her eyes flashed to his face. That curious flicker was in his eyes again; he was watching her with an intensity that was unnerving.

She swung away from him. Why had she lost herself that way? She never did; she was always in control, it was one of the things she prided herself on.

"Go on," he said, his voice surprisingly soft. "I am listening."

Caroline took a deep breath, fixed a polite smile to her face, and turned to face him.

"Look, I'm flattered you think my presence might help your grandmother." Her smile softened. "I like her. Very much. But—I can't stay, Nicolo, even if I'd like to."

"And would you like to? If it were possible, I mean?"

Would she like to stay here, in this beautiful house? Would she like to spend her days with a woman who had already claimed a bit of her heart? Would she prefer that to shimmying down another catwalk?

Caroline sighed. What was the harm in admitting it? Staying on here was about as possible as flying to the moon.

"Sure. If it were possible. But it isn't."

"Because?"

"We've just been through all that! I'm under contract to the agency. I even owe them money. For my rent, for the funds they advance us—"

"Silvio says what you earned modeling for Fabbiano last night paid that off."

She laughed. "That's what he told you. If I were to ask him, the answer would be—"

"It would be the same." Nicolo's expression hardened. "Otherwise, as I explained to him, he would have to answer the question yet again, this time for my attorneys."

"Thank you for that." Sighing, she sank into a chair, and slipped off one shoe, and rubbed her toes against the cool marble floor. "Maybe now I can start out even on the remaining six months of my contract."

Nicolo looked at her in silence, and then he walked to where he'd left his glass of sherry and picked it up.

"What would you say if I told you I could make your contract disappear?"

Her lips curved up in a smile. "I'd say you'd been sitting out in the sun too long."

He lifted the glass to his mouth. "It is simple enough to do," he said, watching her across the rim.

"So is getting sunstroke."

Nicolo frowned. "I am not joking, Caroline."

"No. And neither am I."

His brows knotted together. "Your contract will end, because I will buy it."

Caroline's smile faded. "You'll what?"

"I will buy it, so that I may have you to myself."

She stabbed her toes into her shoe and got to her feet. "Thank you for reminding me of what this is really all about," she snapped. "What is it that the Roman poet Catullus said? 'Hail and farewell'? Well, 'hail and farewell,' Prince—!"

She cried out as he caught her by the shoulders. His eyes had gone from sapphire to a blue so dark it was almost black.

"I told you, I am asking you to be my grandmother's companion."

"Who are you kidding? You'll be damned if you won't try to get me into your bed, one way or another."

Her breath caught as his hands tightened on her. "I assure you, I have no interest in having you in my bed." His mouth twisted, as if he'd tasted something unpleasant. "I have no interest in a woman who prefers herself to anyone else."

"What?"

"Some men may see it as a challenge," he said coldly. "But I do not."

Caroline met his gaze with defiance. "Has anyone ever told you," she said, just as coldly, "that you are the most egotistical man in Rome?"

His eyes darkened again. "Yes," he said. "Someone did. The same someone who taught me that there is no pleasure in a woman's coldness. It made as little impression on me then as it does now."

Arianna, Caroline thought in amazement, they were talking about Arianna again.

His hands tightened on her for an instant, and then he let her go. "So," he said briskly. "What will you do? Will you leave here—or will you stay?"

Her shoulders slumped. "Nicolo, please. You make it sound so simple. But—"

"I will pay you twice the hourly fee you make model-ing—with a guarantee of four months' wages, no matter how quickly the Princess recovers. And, of course, your room and board will be free."

She stared at him. Four months, at double pay, with no charges for rent or food.

"I have to admit, it's tempting," she said with a little laugh. "But even if I were willing to consider it, the agency wouldn't agree to—"

"It already has."

"What do you mean, it already has? Did you discuss this with Silvio without first discussing it with me?"

"Certainly." His smile matched his voice. "There was no reason to tell you of my proposal until I'd assured myself of his agreement to it."

Caroline laughed in disbelief. "If anyone had told me Italy was like this—"

"And what is that supposed to mean?"

"Italian men treat women as if. . . as if they're either creatures who aren't fit to do anything but cook, clean, and have babies—or expensive toys to play with."

"For a woman who claims to have had little to do with my countrymen," Nicolo said coldly, "you seem very well in-formed."

"I'm getting a firsthand lesson! Just look at what you're doing!"

"Yes? What am I doing, Caroline, except offering you a way out of a situation you claim to abhor?"

Caroline rolled her eyes to the ceiling. "I *do* abhor it! But that doesn't mean I want you to—to take over my life. I don't like it. I don't want to be treated as if—as if—"

"I am treating you as you need to be treated," Nicolo said sternly. "*Santa Maria*! Just listen to yourself! Five minutes ago you were ranting about how you hate your work and yet, when I offer you a perfectly equitable way out of your situation, you hesitate."

"I'm not hesitating," Caroline said, folding her arms across her breasts. She gave him a cold look. "I'm turning you down, flat."

"For what reason? Do you think my proposal impossible to carry out?"

"I never said it was impossible. I said—"

"You said, if you could stay here, in Roma, and be *la Principessa*'s companion instead of cavorting on a catwalk, you would leap at the chance."

"That's putting it a little strongly!"

"I think not. Or are you going to claim I misunderstood you?"

Caroline stared at him. The man was worse than she'd thought, not just egocentric but mad, to boot.

"Well?" he demanded. "What are you thinking?"

That you're crazy, she thought, and, without warning, she began to laugh.

Nicolo's eyes narrowed. "If I have misused another of your American idioms," he said stiffly, "I should like to be so informed."

"It isn't that. It's—it's..." Words failed her, and she shook her head. "You just don't see what you've done, do you? Thanks to you, I'm unemployed, penniless, in danger of losing my visa—and there you stand, with that look on your face—"

"Look? What look?"

"The one that says you own the world and all that's in it, that says you can't for the life of you figure out why I'm not jumping for joy at the prospect of staying on here, in this house, as your grandmother's companion."

"You are correct."

Caroline blinked. "I am?"

He nodded. "Now that you point it out, I see that I may have acted precipitately."

She stared at him. "You did?"

"I suppose I should have given you the choice before I took matters into my own hands."

Her eyes narrowed with suspicion. Was he really saying these things? Was he apologizing?

"Certainly it cannot be easy, choosing between slave's wages and a handsome salary."

Caroline shrugged. "Well," she began, "I—"

"Nor can it be any easier to decide if you prefer strolling the runway you abhor or sitting in the garden of the *palazzo*, sipping tea and talking with *la Principessa*."

"Wait a second, Nicolo. You can't just—"

"Undoubtedly, you would have to think a long while before knowing which you prefer."

"You're deliberately oversimplifying things. It's not a matter of which I prefer, it's—"

"As for the rest—I would imagine your living accommodation in Milano must surely outshine the humble comforts of my home." She looked up sharply, in time to see his mouth twitch. "That is right, isn't it?"

"If you're trying to make fun of me..." she said angrily.

Her words faded into the silence. He *was* laughing, but who could blame him? She was being foolish. Ridiculous. She was—

"Caroline." He came toward her and looked into her eyes. "If you truly regret what you left behind in Milano, if you prefer it to what I offer you here, then I will have you flown back there first thing in the morning."

She couldn't help but smile back at him. What he was saying now was tinged with gentle humor, but it was absolutely logical. What woman in her right mind would choose what she'd left in Milan to what he was offering her here, in Rome?

And what was stopping her from accepting that offer? Yes, she'd been worried about Nicolo's intentions, but he'd gone out of his way to tell her—to *show* her—that he wasn't the least bit interested in her as a woman. And heaven knew, she wasn't interested in him. What had happened hours ago, a lifetime ago, when he'd kissed her, had been nothing but an aberration. He'd caught her by surprise, that was all. It hadn't meant a thing.

"Caroline?"

She looked up at him. He was still smiling, a charming, guileless smile that made him appear even more handsome than he already was. Her heart gave an unsteady lurch. Somehow, it was easier to deal with him when he was being intolerably arrogant and demanding than—than—

"Have you reached a decision?" His hands tightened on hers. "Will you stay?"

Caroline took a deep breath. "All right," she said with a hesitant smile. "I—I'll give it a try."

His eyes went dark and, for an instant, the soft, boyish smile became something else, something darker and far more dangerous. But then he laughed, raised her hands to his lips, and lightly put his lips to the back of each.

"Grazie, cara," he said. "Thank you. You will not regret the choice you've made."

She watched as he walked to his desk, reached across it, and pressed a button. Almost immediately, there was a light knock at the door.

"Avanti," Nicolo called out.

The door opened. A girl wearing a white cap and apron stepped inside, cast a shy glance at Caroline, and bobbed her head in a swift but unmistakable gesture of obeisance.

"Eccellenza?"

Nicolo spoke to her. His tone was polite, but there was something about the scene—the girl with her eyes on the ground, the man with the imperious bearing—that set Caroline's teeth on edge. It was an all too chilling reminder of who Nicolo Sabatini really was.

"I have told Lucia to show you to the Teresa de Vertù suite." He smiled. "You will like it, I think. Legend has it that the Queen of—"

"Does Lucia speak any English?"

"She does not. But she is well trained, and—"

"Oh, yes, she is that," Caroline said, very pleasantly. "I saw the little curtsy she made to you—it must be difficult to get people to do that in the 1990s."

Nicolo's smile took on a faint edge. "Did you have something you wished to communicate to the girl, Caroline?"

She nodded. "Please tell her I'll have dinner in my room."

"You will dine at my table."

She looked at Nicolo. He was still smiling, but not enough to obscure the sudden flatness in his eyes.

"I'm tired, Nicolo. I'd much rather have something light in—"

He spoke rapidly to the girl, who bobbed her head again before she turned and left the room. Once she was gone, he looked at Caroline.

"The cook will prepare whatever you wish," he said quietly. "But you will have it at my table."

Caroline jammed her hands into the deep pockets of her skirt. "Is this how it's going to be?" she said. "You're going to give orders, and I'm expected to jump?"

He looked at her for a long moment, and then he walked slowly toward her. When he was a breath away, he stopped, lifted his hand, and touched it gently to her cheek.

"You don't have to jump, *cara*," he said with a little smile. "It will be sufficient if you simply do as you are told."

Before she could move back, he bent and gave her a light, lingering kiss on her mouth. Then he turned on his heel and strode from the room.

CHAPTER SEVEN

HUMMING SOFTLY, Caroline made her way up the broad stairway to the second floor of the *palazzo*. Sunlight streamed through the arched windows, dusting her with pale gold as she hurried along the Aubusson carpet that stretched the length of the gallery. When she reached her bedroom, she opened the door, crossed quickly to the vanity table, and snatched up her sunglasses. Then she retraced her steps, pausing, as she so often did, when she reached the landing.

How beautiful this house was! Even after two weeks, she was still entranced by it. She looked from the magnificent Renaissance oil paintings that graced the wall behind her to the perfect symmetry of the mosaic floor in the atrium.

"The experts say it dates to the first century," Anna Sabatini had said when she'd noticed Caroline admiring it. "It comes from a villa in the hills outside the city. They were going to destroy it, can you imagine? It broke my heart when I heard, and Nicolo—oh, he was so upset! The floor is too beautiful to suffer such a fate, he said." Anna had dropped her voice to a whisper. "It must have cost a fortune to have it taken apart piece by piece and reconstructed, but my Nico never hesitated. Wasn't that good of him?"

Caroline had smiled and said yes, it was, but what she'd really wanted to say was that she doubted if Nicolo had ever hesitated about getting what he wanted in his entire life. He had been born to money, power, and good looks; with a combination like that at his command, why would he hesitate about anything? The world was his. Just look at how he'd arranged her life to suit his plans.

But she hadn't said any of that. She had no wish to hurt Anna and besides, how could she complain when the truth was that she was happier here at the *palazzo* than she'd been in a long time? Perhaps it had something to do with Anna, whom she'd come to love, or with the serenity and beauty of the palace. Caroline sighed. As for her concerns about Nicolo—they'd proven groundless.

She had seen little of him in the first two days. He never put in an appearance until early evening and, except for that first night, he had not even been home for dinner.

"You will forgive me, Caroline," he'd said. "I have not had the time to devote to business lately, but now that my grandmother is feeling better..."

"You don't owe me any explanations," Caroline had answered politely, although she'd wanted to laugh in his face because he'd made his little speech at nine in the evening, dressed in a dinner suit on his way out of the door. Did he think she was a fool? What sort of business did a man conduct at that hour, dressed like that?

Not that she gave a damn. Anything that kept her from running into Nicolo Sabatini was absolutely fine, which was why she had been delighted a few mornings later at the breakfast table when he'd told her he would be away for a few days. Finding him there, waiting for her, had been a surprise. No, that wasn't the right word. It had been—disorienting. There was something about seeing him that way, first thing in the morning, dressed as she'd never seen him before, in a cotton knit shirt and snug, faded jeans, that had made her throat tighten. In fact, if he hadn't looked up from his coffee and spotted her in the doorway, Caroline might have returned to her room and waited until she was sure he'd gone.

But he did look up; those eyes that were the color of a summer sea had moved slowly over her before returning to her face.

"Good morning, Caroline."

She nodded and strode briskly to the sideboard, where she busied herself pouring coffee. "Good morning."

"Good morning, *Nicolo*."

She swung around and looked at him. "Pardon me?"

His smile was slow, almost lazy. "I have noticed," he said softly, "that you do not use my name when you speak to me."

Caroline's eyes met his. "Don't be silly," she said, but she felt her cheeks flame. He was right; she didn't use his name, if she could avoid it. If only there were some compromise between calling him Your Excellency and calling him Nicolo...

He laughed softly. "I can hear you thinking again, *cara*. How much easier it would be if you could refer to me as *Signor* Sabatini, yes?"

It wasn't easy, but she forced herself to go on meeting that blue gaze without flinching.

"Yes—if you'd permit it."

Nicolo shook his head. "I would not."

"No." Caroline picked up her cup and saucer. "I didn't think you would. You much prefer that title of yours to—"

"I much prefer that the woman who lives with me call me by my name."

"I do not live with you," she snapped, which was, of course, exactly what he'd wanted her to do, because he began to grin the second the angry disclaimer left her mouth.

Caroline turned her back to him. Stop being a fool, she told herself angrily. This was a game she couldn't win. He was an experienced womanizer; word games and *double entendres* were second nature to him. But they weren't to her. She'd never been comfortable trading sallies with men. The only way to deal with him was to fall back on the technique that had always served her best. Men who were turned on by a pretty face were turned off by an absolute show of disdain—and if double meanings weren't her strength, turning a cold shoulder was.

"You're right," she said, swinging around to face him. Her expression, and tone, were as neutral as she could manage. "I am living under your roof and accepting wages from you. It's only right I oblige you and address you as you prefer, Nicolo."

His smile never wavered, but she saw a fractional darkening in his eyes.

"Thank you."

She smiled politely. "You're welcome. And now, if that's all . . . ?"

"It is not." He put down his coffee cup. When he looked at her again, his expression was serious, almost stern. "My grandmother is much improved. I see the change, and the *medico* confirms it."

Caroline nodded. This was safer territory.

"I think so, too. Did she tell you she spent yesterday afternoon in the garden with me?"

Nicolo leaned back in his chair and steepled his fingers against his lips. "As I told you, I've had some business to attend to."

It was hard not to smirk. "Oh, yes, I can imagine."

"Can you? It has not been easy, Caroline, fulfilling all my commitments while staying close to the Princess's side."

Caroline smiled sweetly. "Indeed."

Nicolo pushed back from the table and got to his feet. "What would you say if I told you I must go away for a week? For ten days, perhaps? I would phone twice a day, and, of course, I would leave you a complete itinerary where I could be reached if you needed me." He frowned. "Would you feel comfortable alone here with *la Principessa*?"

"Alone? With Signora Brescia living in? With the cook, the gardener, the housekeeper and the maid in the other wing? With the doctor paying daily visits?"

His frown became a smile. "You will not miss me, then?"

"In a word, no."

If she'd hoped to insult him, she didn't succeed. Nicolo only laughed.

"I cannot get used to it, Caroline. That such a beautiful woman should have a tongue dipped in acid still comes as a shock."

"What still comes as a shock," she said with a toss of her head, "is that I'm impervious to your charm."

It had been a stupid thing to say. She knew it as soon as the words left her mouth. Caroline smiled crookedly as he came slowly toward her; her heart leaped into her throat but she stood her ground.

"A challenge, *cara*?" he said softly.

"Not at all. A statement of fact."

He looked at her for a long moment, and then he reached out and slid his hand under her hair, around the nape of her neck. When he spoke, his voice was very low.

"You know that there is unfinished business between us, Caroline."

The same sort of "business" that was taking him away for ten days. Caroline's mouth tightened.

"The only business between us is our agreement regarding my role as companion to your grandmother."

Nicolo smiled. "I know I am right," he said softly. The pressure of his hand increased as he moved nearer to her, so that she had no choice but to let him tip her face up to his. "There is a flame burning within you. That glacial exterior only makes a man the more eager to find it."

They were close, so close, separated only by a breath...

"I seem to recall you telling me you took no pleasure in a woman's coldness," she said with more assurance than she felt.

His thumb stroked across her cheek. "Perhaps you are not as cold as you seem, *cara*."

"Here's an American expression you can add to your collection, Nicolo. What you see is what you get."

He laughed, bent his head, and brushed his mouth lightly against hers. The touch of it electrified her, but she gave no sign.

"Why do I know instinctively that that does not mean that you are willing to admit you burn for me, *cara*?"

Her eyes met his. "Because you know that I don't."

"What I know," he said, touching his lips to her hair, "is that you won't admit it." His other hand came up and cupped her cheek, so that her face was offered up to his. "But you do burn, *carina*," he whispered. "I see the flame in your eyes."

Caroline's heart was racing, but then, why wouldn't it? The man was an accomplished seducer, there was no doubt about it. Even she, who'd been propositioned by experts, had to admit that. His technique was extraordinary, but not extraordinary enough to make her forget reality.

"What you see," she said with a careless smile, "are tears of boredom. This conversation has—"

She never finished the taunting rejoiner. Nicolo's mouth captured hers in a slow, insolent kiss. When he let go of her, she fell back against the sideboard, clutching it for support, fighting for enough composure that she could make some clever response that would make clear that the kiss had not disturbed her in the least.

But he did not give her the opportunity.

"I will see you in ten days, *cara*," he said softly. "And then we will decide which of us is right."

She'd got her voice back too late to answer, she thought now as she remembered the incident. Otherwise, she'd have gone after him, told him it wasn't a matter of right or wrong, it was a matter of when he'd admit he was an arrogant, overbearing liar.

She, burn for him? Ridiculous! It was Nicolo who was obsessed, so obsessed that he'd insisted his only reason for urging her to give up her job and stay here was so she could help his grandmother get well.

It was just too bad she'd been fool enough to believe him.

Caroline's mouth tightened as she made her way past the library, where a copy of his itinerary lay propped beside the telephone. Why he was so intent on seducing her was beyond her comprehension. God knew he had enough "business" to keep him occupied. He'd spent the last few days bouncing from resort to resort. A tennis club in Spain. A yachting club on the Italian coast. A holiday condominium on the Riviera.

Oh, yes, she thought as she stabbed her sunglasses onto her nose, then flung open the doors that led to the garden, Nicolo Sabatini was catching up on his business, all right. No wonder he'd been so eager to sign her on as Anna's companion. He loved the old woman, Caroline admitted grudgingly. But he was also a healthy adult male with an appetite for life, an appetite he was accustomed to feeding, and he'd been hungry for too long. With her here to keep *la Principessa* happy, he could slip the leash and enjoy himself a bit—and if he could seduce her into his bed in between times, so much the better.

She paused when she reached Anna, and a smile softened her face. The Princess was still asleep on her chaise longue, tucked beneath a mohair throw. With a little sigh, Caroline settled into a chair opposite and put her head back.

How peaceful it was here. Outside the high stone walls that encircled the garden, tourists marched the cobbled streets, fought their way through the crowds to see Rome's fabled attractions. But Caroline thought there were enough attractions here, in this quiet place, to last a lifetime. Cypresses grew alongside the walls. Crushed stone paths wound through the beds of early spring flowers to the garden's heart, where a fierce bronze wolf stood guard over an almost magical fountain, water cascading from its mouth into a reflecting pool with a soft, musical murmur. It was the only sound Caroline could hear on this unusually warm afternoon.

"The heat is nothing like it will be during the summer," Anna had warned that morning.

But it was enough to make all the garden's inhabitants drowsy, Caroline thought, yawning. She stretched out her legs, bare beneath a white cotton skirt, opened the first few buttons of her blouse, and fanned herself lightly. Even the pair of plumed cockatoos that normally chattered away at each other in their wrought-iron enclosure were asleep on their perches.

The Princess stirred and murmured something in her sleep. Caroline leaned forward and took her hand.

"Anna?" she said softly. "Are you having a bad dream?"

The old woman sighed as she opened her eyes. "Have I been asleep long?"

Caroline shook her head. "No, not at all. How are you feeling?"

"Better than I have in a long time." Anna smiled again. "Better than an old woman has a right to feel."

"You're not old," Caroline said, patting Anna's hand.

"Of course I am! But I don't feel it, thanks to you. I was right when I said having you here would do more for me than all the medicines in the world." Her fingers tightened on Caroline's. "I am so happy you like it here, child."

"Who wouldn't like it here?" Caroline said gently.

The old woman shrugged expressively. "Some young women might find the life we live here unexciting. You do not miss—how do you say it?—*la dolce vita*?"

Caroline laughed. "Rome isn't exactly the sticks."

"Ah, but you have seen nothing of our city." Anna smiled. "We will change all that when Nicolo returns."

"That's all right," Caroline said, carefully. "I mean, I'm sure the city's beautiful, but—"

"It is unfortunate he had to leave so soon after your arrival."

It wasn't unfortunate at all. On the contrary. It was wonderful. It would be even more wonderful if he called and said he was staying away another week.

"My poor Nico. He works so hard, but what can he do?" Anna yawned. Her voice grew soft and drowsy. "It is not easy, to bear the responsibilities of the Sabatini name..."

The old woman's eyelids drooped, and she began snoring gently. After a bit, Caroline sighed, took off her sunglasses, and closed her eyes, too. Oh, yes, she thought, poor, poor Nicolo. He'd be on the Riviera by now, bearing all those heavy Sabatini responsibilities. So many restaurants to dine at. So many yachts to sail.

So many women to make love to.

Caroline's breath caught. In her mind's eye, she could see him walking out of the velvet sea, the sunlight golden on his skin.

No. No, it would be night, with a full moon casting an ivory pathway over the beach, a pathway leading Nicolo to a woman who stepped from the shadows and held out her arms. He'd go to her, gather her to him so that she felt the hardness of him against her.

"*Cara*," he'd whisper, and the woman would rise on her toes, clasp his face in her hands, and press her mouth to his.

"Nico," she'd sigh, as he drew her down to the sand, "my Nico."

"Caroline?"

Caroline's throat tightened. Yes. That was how he'd say her name, making it into something musical and wonderful, making it—

Her eyes flew open, and her cheeks blazed. Nicolo was standing beside her, his face very still.

"What do you dream of," he said softly, "that brings such a flush to your face?"

"I—I wasn't dreaming. I was just..."

She couldn't speak, not with him looking at her that way. Where had he come from? How long had he been standing there? Her gaze flew over him, taking in the deep, deep blue eyes, the faint smile on the sensual mouth, the dark hair that curled lightly over his collar. He had taken his jacket off; it trailed over one shoulder, held in the hook of one finger. His sleeves were rolled back to reveal golden, muscular forearms, the first two buttons of his shirt were undone so that she could see the strong, tanned column of his throat, the hollow where his pulse beat, the start of the strong, hard planes of his chest.

Caroline sat up quickly and put her hands to her cheeks. "It's—it's impossibly warm today," she said with a little laugh. "Anna warned me about sitting out in the sun, but..." She cleared her throat and looked up at him. "What are you doing here?"

He grinned as he tossed his jacket onto a chair. "I live here, *cara*. Or have you managed to put that unpleasant thought out of your mind?"

Caroline got to her feet. "You said you'd be gone a week, perhaps longer."

"And now here I am." He made a mocking little bow. "Forgive me. I finished my business sooner than I expected."

Her brows lifted. "Really," she said coolly. "What's the matter? Wasn't the weather good on the Riviera?"

He gave her a long look, and then he laughed. "How perceptive of you, *cara*. It wasn't, no. Two days of rain spoiled all my plans."

She nodded. "I'd imagine it would." There was a moment's silence. "Well," she said, briskly, "Anna's going to be very happy to see you. She was just saying that—"

"Actually," he said softly, "I was glad to come home early."

"To see Anna?"

He smiled in a way that made her heart stop beating. "To put our little wager to the test."

"What wager? I don't..."

Their eyes met, and Caroline flushed. "We didn't make a wager," she said quickly.

Nicolo laughed softly. "Perhaps we should have. Let me see. What stakes would be interesting?"

The silence, and the heat, seemed suddenly almost oppressive. Nicolo's eyes dropped to her blouse, and suddenly she was aware of the half-opened neckline. Quickly, fingers trembling, she closed the buttons.

"Dammit," she whispered, "you promised! You said—"

He caught her arm and drew her back under the cypresses. "I know what I said. *Santa Maria*, we both said a lot of things." His hand slid up her arm and he stepped closer to her. "Now," he said, very softly, "I think, perhaps, it is time to say other things."

Caroline shook her head. "There's nothing left to say, Nicolo."

He smiled. "I think there is, *cara*," he whispered.

He bent and kissed her, and the world shifted out from under her feet. How could she have remembered the taste of his mouth? He had only kissed her a few times before, yet his taste was as familiar as the beat of his heart beneath her hand as she clutched his shirt.

Was she clutching his shirt? She was. She was holding on for dear life, leaning into him, lifting on tiptoe so that he could gather her close, hold her tightly in his arms, while his tongue slipped into her mouth, while his hand swept up her ribs and lightly cupped her breast...

Caroline slammed her hands against his chest and thrust herself free of his embrace.

"You—you bastard!" she hissed.

"*Cara*, listen to me..."

"No!" She stepped backward and shook her head. "No, Nicolo, you listen to me for a change. I—I'm not proud of what just happened."

"Caroline, please—"

"It—it disgusts me to think that I'd let you kiss me that way."

Darkness filled his eyes. "Disgusts you?" he said slowly.

No, she thought. That was the wrong word. It—it frightened her. It terrified her, that she could so lose control in the arms of this man who was everything she despised, who despised her, who wanted her for what he thought she was.

His hands tightened on her. "My kiss disgusts you?"

Her eyes flew to his. What could she say that would make sense? What could she say that would not reveal her vulnerability, a vulnerability that she, herself, could not explain?

Nicolo's nostrils flared. "I see." His hand fell away from her. "In that case—"

"Nico?" Nicolo and Caroline spun around. Anna Sabatini was rising from her chair, her face beaming with pleasure. "Nico, *caro*, you're home!"

Nicolo's face underwent a transformation. *"Nonna."* He stepped forward, bent, and embraced the old woman lovingly. Then he eased her back onto the chaise longue and gave her a stern look. "Have you behaved yourself while I was away?"

Anna made a face. "I've been a perfect angel. Caroline will tell you. I have done nothing but sleep too much, eat too much, and sit in the sun and bake!" She smiled. "The doctor says I'm fine. He says you can stop treating me like an invalid."

"I know. I spoke with him this morning."

"Well, then, we must celebrate!" Anna reached out her hands, one to Caroline, one to Nicolo. "You must shower and change, Nico, and then—what shall we do?"

He smiled. "Whatever you like."

"Really?" The Princess's pale eyes gleamed. "Do you mean that?"

"Of course" He looked at Caroline. "Caroline and I are yours to command."

Anna looked at Caroline. "Do you agree?"

Caroline smiled. "Of course."

"In that case...I think first, the view of the city from the Pincio. Or perhaps a visit to the Fontana di Trevi." Anna made a face. "Soon, it will be impossible to see, because of the tourists, but, for now, the city still belongs to us Romans.''

Nicolo nodded thoughtfully. "If the weather is cooler later in the week, perhaps, we can do one or the other. I shall have your driver bring your car around and—''

"Then the Forum. And the Colosseum. Oh, and the Baths of Caracalla.''

A slow smile eased across his mouth. "Ah, I see. You have a week's journey in mind, yes?''

"And we must not forget the Pantheon. And the Vatican Museums, of course.''

Nicolo laughed. "Of course.''

"It will be late by then, a good time for Campari and soda at some out-of-the-way café.'' She pursed her lips. "As for dinner... what do you think, Nico? Is that restaurant still near the Spanish Steps, the one that serves that superb *vongole veritas*? Or do you think Caroline would prefer somewhere more intimate?''

"Not one week's journey.'' Nicolo grinned. "This is a two-week plan.''

"And finally, a stroll around our very own *plazza*, to see the fountains by moonlight.'' She looked up at Caroline. "How does that sound, dear? You would like to see all that, wouldn't you?''

Caroline smiled. "Don't you think you should begin with a lighter schedule?''

La Principessa drew back in mock horror. "I? You think I want to go to all those places?'' She shuddered. "Not at *my* age.'' A sly smile curved across her lips. "But you—and Nico—will have a wonderful time.''

Caroline's smile vanished. She looked quickly at Nicolo and saw that his smile had fled, too. He was watching her with that same intensity she'd seen in his face before, the one that made his eyes seem like dark sapphires.

"No," she said without thinking, "no. I don't want to go with...'' Her words faded to silence. She saw Nicolo's jaw tighten. "I mean, who would stay with you, Anna?''

"Caroline is right, *Nonna*.'' Nicolo's voice was flat and chill. "If she wishes to play at being a tourist, I will arrange for a guide for her.''

Anna looked from one to the other and shook her head. "Such nonsense! I do not need you to stay with me, Caroline. You yourself pointed out that the *palazzo* is filled with people. And Nicolo. Surely a guide would be helpful, but only if you are at Caroline's side, as well. Who else could tell her as much about our beloved *Roma*?"

"I have just stepped off the plane, *Nonna*. What I want most just now is a long shower and—"

"But of course, Nico! You must shower while Caroline changes to something cool. A sundress, perhaps. Oh, and low-heeled sandals, if you have them. Do you, dear?"

Caroline blew out her breath. "Yes, but—"

"Well, then, go and make yourselves ready." Anna smiled happily.

Nicolo lifted his head. His eyes met Caroline's. They were cool and unreadable, as was his face.

"Be ready in half an hour," he said coldly.

Anna Sabatini, oblivious to everything, sighed. "I just know you're going to have a wonderful time!"

NOT EVEN THE MOST dedicated tourist could have managed to complete Anna's travel plan, although Nicolo was certainly giving it a determined try. He wove his Ferrari in and out of traffic with an abandon that kept Caroline pinned back in her seat.

"The Arch of Constantine," he growled, as they zoomed by an enormous triumphant monument. "It was built in honor of the Emperor Constantine in the fourth century."

She peered out the window, but they were already past it.

"The Colosseum," Nicolo said, jamming the car into a lower gear as they approached a snarl of traffic. "Built by the Emperor Vespasian in A.D. 72." The tires squealed as the Ferrari shot forward. "It is where the Christian martyrs met their deaths, and where wild animals and gladiators battled for the pleasure of the city's populace."

Caroline peered out again. The Colosseum was huge and wonderful to behold, even though much of its decorative sculpture had been stolen over the centuries for the building of many of Rome's palaces. She knew that much from the English-language books she'd read during the evenings, sitting in the Sabatini library. What she longed to do was get out and walk through the ancient amphitheater—but, clearly, that was not going to happen.

"Il Foro Romano," Nicolo said as they shot by a clutch of tumbled white marble ruins. "The Roman Forum."

Caroline stared back over her shoulder. The Forum, she thought longingly, where Caesar spoke to the Senate.

"You may have heard of it in history class in school."

She looked at Nicolo. "I suppose," she said, "if I try very hard, I might recall some reference." ·

"And the Campidoglio," he said, ignoring the sarcasm of her response. "It was the Capitol in ancient times, and the smallest of the seven hills of Rome. Michelangelo designed the ceremonial ramp and staircase that leads to the summit."

Caroline shaded her eyes. "Is that where Roman generals marched in celebration? To the Campidoglio, from the Via Sacra?"

Nicolo looked at her. "What?"

"Did I pronounce it wrong? The Via Sacra. The Sacred Way. It was the route of triumph for—"

"I know what it was," he said coldly. "I am only surprised that *you* know of it."

Caroline smiled tightly. "Did you think I was incapable of memorizing anything but my own measurements?"

He looked at her again. For just an instant, she thought he was going to smile and say, "All right, Caroline, this isn't so terrible after all. I don't mind taking you on this silly tour, in fact, I think I might just enjoy it."

But then his mouth tightened again, and he looked away. Caroline slumped back in her seat. Why on earth would he ever say such a thing to her? He had never made a secret of what he wanted from her, and pretending he enjoyed her company, pretending he wanted to laugh with her or show her his favorite places in Rome, wasn't part of it.

What was the matter with her? She didn't want to be with him, any more than he wanted to be with her. The tension of being in his company had to be getting to her. Dammit, this was infuriating!

"I give you your choice of what to see next." She looked over at him. He was staring straight ahead, his eyes fixed to the road. "The Via Veneto? The Baths of Carcalla? The Circus Maximus?"

"Why don't we do ourselves a favor?" she said through her teeth. "You let me out at the next corner. I'll buy a guide book, go see some stuff, kill a couple of hours while you go plop yourself down somewhere cool and shady and have a beer or whatever this season's trendy drink is, and then we'll meet at six o'clock or so, ride back to the palace together, and tell Anna we had an absolutely smashing day." She paused for effect. "How's that sound?"

"Perfect." Nicolo shot her a cold smile. "Except for one or two minor problems."

"For instance?"

"For instance, we can't show our faces at the *palazzo* until at least eleven tonight." He gave her another terrible smile. "Children dine at six. Romans have their evening meal at nine. Whatever you may think of us, Caroline, we are not children."

"Meaning Americans are?"

Nicolo sighed. "Look. I'm no happier doing this than you are. But since we're stuck to each other for the next several hours—"

"Stuck *with* each other," Caroline snapped. "If you can't get those expressions right, why do you insist on using them?"

Nicolo's jaw shot forward. "Perhaps for the same reason I foolishly asked you to stay with Anna in the first place," he snarled. "Because it seemed like a good idea at the time."

"Ha!" Caroline swung away and stared out the windshield.

"Ha?" Nicolo's brows lifted. "What does 'ha' mean, if you don't mind my asking?"

"It means," she said coldly, "that you asked me to stay with Anna because you thought you could seduce me."

"By the bones of my ancestors!" Nicolo slammed his hand on the steering wheel. "Are we back to that again?"

She spun around to face him. "Are you going to try and deny it? You've done nothing but hit on me since the day—"

"Hit?" He glared at her. "I have never, in my life, hit a woman. Any woman. Not even one as impossible as you."

"It's an expression, for God's sake! It means you've—you've been coming on to me . . ." His brows rose and Caroline puffed out her breath. "I told you, right from the start, that I wasn't interested."

"Yes." His tone was grim. "You made that most clear today."

"I hope so."

"Don't worry. I am not so thick-brained that I didn't get the memo."

"Thick-skulled," she said. "What you mean is, you're not so thick-skulled that you didn't get the message."

Nicolo shrugged stiffly. "It is the same thing."

"It isn't. You—you . . ." Caroline stared at him, then shook her head wearily and lay it back on the seat. "You just don't understand."

"Oh, but I do." He shot her a cold look. "We are trapped together for the day."

She sighed. "I'm afraid we are."

"Then I suggest we do the best we can for the next several hours. We shall see Rome with a guide, we will be polite to each other, and, eventually, the day will end. Will you agree?"

Caroline sighed again. Did she have a choice?

"I agree."

His jaw tightened. "So be it."

He jammed his foot down on the accelerator and the car shot forward.

CHAPTER EIGHT

CAROLINE AND Nicolo stood inside the Pantheon with their guide, a little man with a pedantic style and a phenomenal level of endurance. He had met them at the Piazza Venezia two hours before. Nicolo had made the arrangements by telephone.

"I will show you all the best of Roma," he'd announced with a modest smile, and, to be kind, Caroline supposed he was trying to do just that.

But she was in no mood for sightseeing, and neither was Nicolo, judging by the look on his face. Not that he'd said so; he hadn't spoken a word to her since the guide had joined them.

It was ridiculous to pretend that either of them gave a damn about columns and arches and treasures of the old world just now. But Nicolo was right. They had no choice. To go back to the *palazzo* would mean having to explain their early arrival to Anna, and how would they manage that?

The thing to do, Caroline told herself, was lose herself in the beauty and lore of Rome, and she might have done that—if the guide had only let her. But he was filled with facts and figures and determined to recite every one, as effective a way as any to silence the whispers of antiquity that danced in the air. Nothing seemed to deter him, not even his audience's lack of response.

"... built in 27 B.C. by Marcus Agrippa, son-in-law of the Emperor Augustus. The dome is forty-three point two meters in diameter. The height of the building is, as well, forty-three point two meters." He smiled, as if he were personally responsible for the perfection of those measurements. "Note, please, the center opening."

Caroline tilted her head obediently.

"The opening, which admits the sun, is nine meters wide. Visitors through the centuries have been impressed by the beauty and harmony of these proportions."

As I would be, Caroline thought, if you'd only be still for a moment.

"Interesting," she said, when she realized he expected a comment.

He nodded and looked at Nicolo. Caroline looked at him, too, and her eyes widened. She might be so bored that her jaw ached from trying not to yawn, but Nicolo—Nicolo looked as if he were about to explode.

He was truly miserable! How nice. She smiled for the first time in hours.

"Very interesting," she said.

The guide looked at Nicolo, whose brows knitted together.

"Yes," he growled. "Interesting."

The guide nodded and set off briskly across the floor.

"Statues of the gods once stood in the niches that surround us, but they were borrowed over the centuries and not returned. I say 'borrowed' because it would be impolite to suggest that anyone might have stolen them." He smiled to show that he'd made a joke.

"Did they, though?" Caroline said.

"Did they what, *signorina*?"

"Steal the statues?"

Unplanned interruptions were not part of his repertoire. His frown made that clear.

Nicolo made an impatient gesture. "Of course they did. Barbarians stole the statues."

"Perhaps, Excellency. Now, if you will follow me—"

"Barbarians stole the statues," Nicolo repeated in a way that made it clear he would accept no argument. "But Urban the Eighth took the bronze from the inside of the dome and gave it to Bernini so he could create a *baldacchino*—a canopy—for the papal altar in Saint Peter's."

Caroline frowned. "How do you know all that?"

"It is public knowledge," Nicolo said arrogantly. "And I have read the story about Bernini in the diaries of Gregorio Sabatini."

"Diaries?" Caroline's face lit. "From the Renaissance?"

"*Sì*. Gregorio was apprentice to Bernini, and—"

"Oh, how exciting! Did he—?"

"I am sure you wish to see the rest of the building," the guide said sternly, and marched off.

Caroline sighed and fell in behind him. After a second, so did Nicolo.

"The portico is thirty-three meters wide and thirteen point five meters high. It has six granite columns with Corinthian capitals that are twelve point five meters in height. They are spaced four—"

"Four point five meters apart," Nicolo snapped.

Caroline and the guide stared at Nicolo, who glowered back. "I remember this from my school books."

"Ah," the guide said with too perfect a smile, "then you may remember, too, that the doors through which we just passed measure seven point three two meters. And that there were once five steps leading to the portico which measured—"

"*Basta!*" The word erupted from Nicolo's throat in a roar.

The guide's eyebrows rose until they almost met his hairline. "Is there a problem, sir?"

Two spots of color rose on Nicolo's cheeks. "No. No problem. It's just..." He dug into his pocket and pulled out a stack of bills. "This should do it."

"But—I don't understand. If the tour has not been satisfactory..."

"No, no, it's been fine! I—I remembered I've an appointment. A meeting." He grabbed the man's hand and stuffed money into it. "And another fifty thousand *lire* as a bonus for all the excellent information you gave us," he said briskly.

The guide gave him a puzzled smile. "It is too much, Excellency. We have not completed our tour."

"Not to worry," Nicolo said with a smile. "I shall call you the next time we are free, and we will do the rest. Yes?"

"Yes, if that is what you wish. But—"

"It is. Absolutely," he said, hooking an arm around the man's shoulders and leading him from the porch. He looked, Caroline thought, like a host taking leave of a guest who'd resisted all efforts to call it an evening. When he returned, she smiled brightly.

"Well," she said, "that was certainly—interesting."

"Yes." He nodded stiffly. "I hope I did not spoil things for you."

"An appointment, hmm?"

His eyes met hers. "I will call and arrange for another guide. If you wish to wait here—"

She couldn't keep from shuddering. "No. No, please, don't!" She hesitated. "I'd just as soon do it without a guide. Is that possible?"

Nicolo glared at her. "I suppose it is. I do know something of this city."

"Well, then ... ?"

"But I am not a professional guide, Caroline."

"I see." She nodded. "You won't be able to tell me the height of the Sistine Chapel?"

"I'm afraid not."

"Nor the number of days it took to build the Palazzo Farnese?"

He shrugged. "I have no idea."

Caroline smiled a little, "But you might know the history of the Farnese family."

"Yes, certainly. In fact, a Farnese married a Sabatini."

"When?"

He shrugged. "Not too long ago. In the late seventeen hundreds or perhaps the early eighteen hundreds."

She sighed happily. "Tell me about it," she said.

He did, while they crossed the *piazza*. By the end of the story, she was laughing.

"Oh, that's so much more interesting than hearing how many tons of marble went into the Arch of Constantine!"

Nicolo chuckled. "I agree. That poor man was impossible."

"Worse than impossible. I had an English teacher like that once. Mrs. Bengs. She was supposed to teach us poetry, but—"

"But all she talked about was meter."

Caroline smiled up at him. "How did you know?"

"Because I suffered through a class on American nineteenth-century poetry with a professor who did the same thing." They stepped off the curb and Nicolo slipped his arm around Caroline's waist as he guided her to the other side of the street. "I'd hoped for so much from that class since I was taking it at an American university, but—"

"What university?"

"Yale."

"You went to Yale?"

"*Sì*. For my undergraduate degree."

She thought of what he'd said about New England that day he'd brought her to Rome, and how arrogantly she'd reacted.

"Then—you do know something about New England," she said slowly.

Nicolo shrugged. "I lived in the northeast for six years, first in Connecticut, then in Pennsylvania. I took my graduate degree at Wharton."

"In business?"

"Of course." He grinned. "Does Wharton give any other kind? Why do you look so surprised, *cara*? It is because I studied in your country—or is it because I studied at all?"

It was Caroline's turn to blush. "I only meant—"

"I am only teasing you, Caroline. Anyway, no matter how much one studies, it is difficult to keep up with changes in the financial world." He gave her a quick, self-deprecating smile. "Yesterday, for instance, at my meeting in Cannes—"

"Cannes?" she repeated foolishly. "You mean, you went there on business?"

Nicolo looked at her as if she'd lost her mind. "Certainly. I told you that before I left." He grimaced. "For months we talked financing with these people. Do they wish to have us back them in their expansion of their resorts in France? On the Italian coast? On the Riviera?" His arm tightened around her as they stepped off the curb again. "They could not decide—and then, all at once, they came to Rome last week and yes, they want money from Sabatini. And they must have an answer from me *subito*."

"You mean, you're in charge?"

Nicolo gave her a searching glance. "And that surprises you too, eh? Ah, *cara*, you are like a sheet of glass. You are so translucent—"

"Transparent."

"What is the difference? The light shines through both, no?"

"No. I mean, yes. But you see right through the one, while the other..."

"While the other you cannot." He gave her a quick smile. "I know the difference, *cara*. But you—you do not."

"Me?" She laughed. "Don't be silly."

"You assumed, from the beginning, that you could see through me."

Caroline flushed. "That's not fair!"

"The playboy prince. Too many women, too much money, and not enough brains to fill a teakettle. Am I right?"

Caroline felt her flush deepening, but she was not going to be the only one under attack here.

"You've got the idiom wrong again," she said. "It's teacup, not teakettle." She looked straight at him. "But it wouldn't have taken even that much to know that nobody is transparent—or translucent."

Nicolo gave a little nod of his head. "I admit, you are not what I thought."

Did he really think he was going to get off that easily? Her chin rose.

"Meaning what, exactly?"

"Meaning," he said, with a little smile, "that I misjudged your morality."

"Yes," she said stiffly. "You certainly did."

"I should not have made such quick assumptions."

"No. You should not."

Nicolo smiled. "You don't give an inch, do you, *cara*?"

"Why should I? You insulted me, you—"

"And I have apologized—which is more than you have done."

Caroline blinked. "Me? But..."

Her words faded to silence. Did she really owe him an apology? Perhaps she did. In her own way, she had been every bit as insulting to him as he'd been to her.

"Caroline?" Nicolo stepped in front of her and smiled. "What do you say? Shall we bury the ax?"

It was impossible not to smile. "The hatchet," she murmured.

He laughed and held out his hand. "We will bury it, no matter what it is called," he said. "Yes?"

She looked at him. His smile was open and friendly, and suddenly it seemed preposterous to be standing here, on a Roman street corner, arguing with a man who had taken her from an existence that she'd hated to one that was all she'd ever dreamed of.

Her smile broadened. "All right," she said, and put her hand in his.

Nicolo raised it to his lips. She barely felt the brush of his mouth against her skin, yet it sent a bolt of electricity shooting through her.

"Then, come, *cara*," he said softly. "And I will show you my city."

THEY WENT BACK to the Forum.

"Seeing it from the car didn't do it justice," Nicolo said.

No, Caroline thought, as she let him lead her down to the ancient ground, no, it hadn't. And she hadn't done Nicolo Sabatini justice, either. She had expected him to know what to whisper to a woman in the heat of passion, not to be able to tell her stories about Alaric, the Goth chieftain who'd conquered Rome in A.D. 410. But that was what he'd been doing for the past several minutes.

"And he burned this basilica—the Basilica Aemilia—almost to the ground. It was a pity, for the Basilica was very old even then."

Caroline looked at the ruins that remained. "What sort of building had it been? A fortress of some kind? A temple?"

"It was a shelter for those who came here to buy and sell their wares." He put his arm around her shoulders as they walked on. "It's named for the man who built it. Marcus Aemilius."

"I see. It was an inn."

Nicolo shook his head. "No, it was a public building, meant to protect merchants and their customers from the elements." He grinned. "Everybody complains about taxes today, but in ancient times wealthy Romans were expected not just to pay their taxes but to finance public works, as well."

Caroline laughed. "Some people might think that's an idea that needs reintroducing. And what's that?" she said, nodding toward another tumble of stone.

"A temple of Venus. The goddess of love." Nicolo smiled. "And at the far end of the street was the Temple of Vesta. Opposite attractions, one might say. The Vestals were sworn to a life of chastity. If they broke their vows..."

He made a sawing gesture across his neck, and Caroline shuddered. "Ugh! How could they get women to sign on for such a life?"

"For one thing, it was an honor." He paused, and she could see laughter dancing in his eyes. "And the girls were given to the priests by their families when they were ten or eleven years old."

"But that's terrible!"

"It's the only way anyone could ensure they'd be virgins!"

They both laughed, and then Caroline swept out her hand. "There's so much to know—how can you remember it all?"

Nicolo took her hand and swung it gently as they walked. "I grew up on these stories. My grandfather was an archaeologist, and—"

"The Princess's husband?"

He nodded. "He was always involved in one dig or another. Sometimes he let me tag along. I loved to hear him talk about the old days."

"The very old days," Caroline said with a smile. "I'm surprised you didn't follow him into archaeology."

"I thought about it, believe me." His fingers laced through hers. "But by the time I was eighteen, I realized that, as much as I loved studying the past, my greatest joy came from—well, I suppose you'd describe it as planning things and watching them grow."

"Ah," Caroline said lightly. "So that's how someone gets to be head of a corporation! He shows a talent for gardening."

Nicolo grinned as he drew her down beside him on a marble bench. "Unfortunately, I have absolutely no talent at all for gardening, *cara*. Anna refers to me as *il pollice nero*. The black thumb." They smiled at each other, and then he reached out and smoothed a strand of hair behind Caroline's ear. "Now it's your turn," he said, "although I suspect I know how a woman gets to be an international model. She starts life as an adorable little girl and grows up to be an extraordinarily beautiful woman."

She shook her head. "Actually, I was a gawky little girl."

"You? No. I don't believe it."

"It's true. I was too tall, too skinny, I had freckles..."

"I like freckles," he said softly.

"My grandmother used to say that, too. She raised me, you see, after my folks died..."

Why was she telling him all this? Why would he care about her childhood, or her grandmother? But he seemed to; he was nodding, his expression serious and intent.

"Yes? It was the same for me." His eyes swept over her face. "Is that why you took such an immediate liking to Anna? Because she reminds you of your own *nonna*?"

Caroline nodded. "She does, a little."

He smiled. "And it was your grandmother who convinced you that you weren't an ugly duckling, that you would grow up to be a swan?"

She laughed. "I suppose that's close enough to the truth." Her smile tilted. "But I never thought about becoming a model. It was only after Grams died..."

Nicolo put his hand under her chin and tilted her face up. "Such a sad face, *cara*. What happened?"

The breath sighed from her lungs. "She'd been ill for a long time. There was no money left." She looked at him.

"And no jobs, not in Chatam, Vermont, at any rate. So I went to New York—and there were no jobs there, either, not unless you had a college degree or you could type a million billion words a minute. And then—"

"And then, one day, a man came up to you on the street." Nicolo's voice took on an almost perfect New York accent. "Hey, kid," he said, "didja ever think of becoming a model?"

Caroline burst out laughing. "Actually, it was a woman. She worked for a modeling agency. But that's just about what she said—and just about the way she said it."

He rose and held out his hand. Caroline took it and they began walking again.

"And so you signed on with International Models?"

"No, not then. I did a couple of years of catalog work— companies that sell clothing through the mail," she said, in answer to his puzzled look. "Sears, Spiegel. Penney's... well, you wouldn't know the names. But the work was steady and the pay was pretty good."

"But not good enough?" he prompted.

She shrugged. "By then, I knew that what I really wanted was to become a designer." She looked at him, her expression almost defiant. "It wasn't really such a sudden decision. I'd always made most of my own clothes, and—"

"I believe it, *cara*," Nicolo said gently.

Caroline sighed. "Sorry. It's just that New York fashion people look down their noses at you unless you're a graduate of a fancy school of design."

"Which is why you decided to try your hand at a kind of modeling that would pay better," he said. "So you could save your pennies and enroll in one of those schools."

She looked at him, surprised. "Did I tell you this before?"

"No," he said, smiling. "But it adds up."

"Yes." She blew out her breath. "I thought so, too. That was why I signed with another agency. I got some better paying work for a while—and then International Models approached me." Her mouth curved into a weary smile. "They made it sound so wonderful..."

"But, in truth, it was hell."

Her head lifted. His voice was grim, his eyes dark and angry.

"No," she said after a moment, "Not hell. I mean, it could have been lots worse." She gave him a long, steady look. "Anyway, now, thanks to you and Anna, I'm out of it."

"Yes. You are, *cara*. And you will not return to that life ever again."

Why was he looking at her that way? As if—as if he knew something she did not? She had seen him like this before, the night they'd met, when he'd been determined to have his own way; she'd seen him like this again, when he'd announced she was not going to return to Milan..."

Caroline shivered.

"*Cara?* What is it? Are you cold?"

"I—I am, a little." She looked up. The crowd had thinned, and the day was coming to an end. The sun was arcing toward the horizon, turning the ancient ruins into a place of magic—a place where not only Romans had once walked, but barbarians, too. Another shudder racked her body. "I guess I didn't realize how late it had gotten."

Nicolo frowned. "Forgive me," he said. "I have kept you talking too long."

"We'd better get back. Anna will be wondering what happened to us."

"What you mean is, she will wonder what happened if we return to the *palazzo* at such an early hour. Have you forgotten, *cara*? We are to have drinks, then dinner, before we show our faces. Believe me, I would sooner go hat in hand to all the bankers in Europe than try and explain to Anna why we'd ignored her imperial command." He grinned as he tucked her hand under his arm. "Do you see what it says everywhere in Rome? On buildings, on pavements, even on post boxes?"

She looked at him and smiled hesitantly. "You mean, 'SPQR'? Yes. I noticed. What does it mean?"

"The Senate, the People, and the Republic. It is an ancient credo that means all Romans are as one." His grin broadened. "But there should be an addendum to it. It should say, 'SPQR—by the grace of Her Highness, the

Princess Sabatini' What she decrees is law." His voice turned soft and cajoling. "Besides, could you say no to Campari and soda at Casina Valadier on the Pincio Hill, where the view goes on forever? Or to dinner at Girone VI, where you will have to decide which is the more perfect, the seventh-century walls—" he smiled "—or the chef's stuffed pasta with walnut sauce."

"Stuffed pasta with walnut sauce?"

"*Sì*. The best you have ever tasted."

Caroline laughed. "You mean, the *only* pasta with walnut sauce I've ever tasted."

"You have led a life of deprivation, *cara*." Nicolo grinned. "And it is my duty to change it."

They smiled at each other, and Caroline felt a strange tightening within her breast. That was just what she was afraid of, she thought suddenly; he had already wrought too many changes, not just in her life, but—but . . .

"Well?" Nicolo put his hands on her shoulders. "What do you think?"

Drinks and dinner, that was all they'd be sharing. And why not, when the afternoon had gone so well?

Caroline took a deep breath. "What I think," she said lightly, "is that I'm starving."

Smiling, Nicolo put his arm around her shoulders and led her back to where they'd left the Ferrari.

NICOLO WATCHED as Caroline spooned the last bit of tiramisu from her dessert plate. When she'd finished, he put down his cup of espresso, propped his elbow on the table and put his chin in his hand.

"Anna would be proud of you," he said, "*Antipasto misto*, the pasta with walnut sauce, *saltimbocca* . . ."

"And each bit probably contained a thousand calories." He nodded. "At least."

"You're not supposed to agree with me, Nicolo!" She grinned. "You're supposed to roll your eyes and assure me that I just had the low-cal, spun-out-of-air version of—whatever all that incredible stuff was."

Nicolo laughed as he lifted his cup of *espresso* to his lips.

"I always imagined models lived on lettuce leaves and iced water."

"They do. Well, I do, anyway. The first agency I went to sent me to a photographer to have some pictures taken for my portfolio. He told me to come back after I'd starved off ten pounds."

"A man?"

She nodded. "He was right, too. You photograph better when—"

"Surely no man—not even a fashion photographer—would want to take away any of those lovely curves."

Nicolo was still smiling, but his voice had become husky. Caroline cleared her throat.

"Actually—actually, that was the first time it occurred to me that no one was designing clothes—beautiful, well-tailored clothes—for real women. And—"

"Is that what you are interested in, *cara*?" He put his cup down again and ran his finger around its thin gold rim. "Being a real woman?"

"I *am* a real woman," she said with a puzzled smile. "I've told you, I hate those insane things people like Fabbiano design, and—"

"I meant, do you hope some day to marry? To have a husband and babies?"

She stared at him. How had the conversation suddenly become so personal?

"I don't know," she said honestly. "I mean, I've never really thought about it."

"Why haven't you?" He smiled very gently. "Surely, a woman as beautiful as you had proposals."

Her head came up sharply. "What is *that* supposed to mean?"

Nicolo's brows lifted. "Only that I cannot believe no man has yet asked you to marry him."

"Oh." Caroline looked down at the table. "Sorry," she said with an apologetic little laugh, "I thought—"

"But there have been men in your life, Caroline. Haven't there?"

She looked at him. He was smiling still, but there was something about the smile that sent a warning tingle dancing along her spine.

What kind of questions were these to ask her? A real woman, indeed! Did he think she was just a face and body, a woman so enamored of herself and her career that she had no emotions?

"Of course there have been men," she said with a toss of her head.

And there had been. One or two, anyway. None who'd ever meant anything, but what business was that of his?

Nicolo leaned forward. "Men," he said pleasantly. "But no commitment." He nodded, as if she'd told him something very clever. "Why is that, hmm?"

The answer was almost painfully simple. Because she'd never fallen in love, the head-over-heels, with-all-your-heart kind of love that made a woman's world center on one man for the rest of her life.

She looked at Nicolo. Why was he looking at her like that, with that little smile that suggested he knew something she did not? She had no wish to strip herself bare for his amusement.

"Well," she said with a shrug, "I've been busy, building my career. I told you, someday I want to be a designer, and—"

"And that is more important than anything else."

Her eyes swept across his face, and suddenly she had the almost overwhelming desire to tell him that it wasn't important at all, that she was, inside, what he'd call a real woman, one who wanted a home and children to fill it, and most of all a husband, a man who would take her in his arms and kiss her until nothing mattered except him, kiss her as Nicolo had, make her want him as she'd wanted Nicolo..."

The suddenness of the realization stole her breath away. What was happening to her? She barely knew this man, and yet—and yet...

"Of course," she said quickly. "Why wouldn't it be?"

"Why, indeed?" His voice was cool, with amusement or perhaps derision. She thought it might be either, but when she looked up, he was smiling pleasantly. "Well." He took some bills from his pocket and tossed them onto the table, then rose to his feet. "I think we've made enough of this day to satisfy even *la Principessa*. Shall we leave?"

They drove back in silence. Something had gone out of the day, Caroline thought, but what? Nicolo had seemed so relaxed; now, he sat beside her, his body stiff with tension. Or with anger, although she couldn't imagine at what.

The *palazzo* was silent when they reached it. Good, Caroline thought. She was in no mood to see Anna; all she wanted was to go to her room and be alone, to think about this strange day and the stranger way it had ended.

"Good night," she said. Her voice quavered a little, and she cleared her throat. "Thank you for—"

Nicolo put his hand on her arm. "Not yet." His voice was tight with tension, but he smiled. "I just remembered—we promised Anna we'd see the *piazza* by moonlight."

"No. No, it's much too late, Nicolo."

"A drink, then. A very small cognac."

"Thank you, but—I just want to go to my room."

His arm slid lightly around her. "Then I'll take you there."

"It isn't necessary..."

But he was already leading her to the stairs. Her heart hammered in her throat. Something was very wrong, she could feel it in her bones, but what was it? At the door, she turned and held out her hand.

"Well, here we are," she said. "Thank you again, Nicolo, for—"

"Did you really enjoy yourself, *cara*?"

"Yes." She smiled a little. "The day couldn't have been lovelier."

"I am glad to hear it."

She nodded. "Well, good—"

"Caroline." He reached out and touched her hair lightly. "Your hair is like silk, *cara*. Soft, golden silk."

Her heart leaped against her ribs. "Nicolo. It's late. And—"

"And your eyes." He cupped her face in his hands. "They are the color of the sea off the Greek Islands."

"Nicolo." Was that tiny voice hers? "Nicolo," she said, "listen—"

"But your mouth..." His thumb traced across her lips, and they parted at his touch. "Ah, *cara*, that perfect mouth."

"Don't, please," she whispered.

"Would you tell me not to touch the little Degas horse that stands on my desk?" His hands slid into her hair and he lifted her face to him. "Then how can you tell me not to taste your mouth, when it is so full and beautiful, when it waits for my kiss."

He bent his head and touched his lips to hers. The kiss was gentle, so soft she barely felt it.

"Sweet," he murmured, "as sweet as I knew it would be." He smiled into her eyes. "Kiss me, *cara*. Just give me one kiss."

One kiss, she thought, while the floor tilted under her feet. One kiss...

His mouth caught hers again, and this time the tip of his tongue stole across her lips. She made a little sound in the back of her throat.

"Caroline," he whispered. "Caroline, *bellissima*... Open your mouth to me, *cara*. Let me taste you."

He lowered his head slowly to hers. She watched as his eyes darkened, as his lashes fell to his cheeks. Her heart was thundering as his lips touched hers. This wasn't supposed to happen—but then, nothing today had happened as it had been supposed to. She had been so certain she'd known all there was to know about the man in her arms—but she hadn't. She hadn't known him at all.

"Caroline. Kiss me back, *cara*. You know it is what you want." He bit lightly at her lower lip. "Give yourself to the night—and to me."

A sob burst from her throat, and she clutched at him fiercely, dragged his head down to hers.

"Nico," she whispered against his mouth, "Nico, please..."

The door swung open behind her, and they slipped into the darkness of her bedroom.

"Yes, *cara*. I am here. Tell me what you want and I will do it."

What *did* she want? His kisses? His caress? Or something more?

She shook her head, buried her face against his shoulder. "I don't—Nico, I don't know. I—"

"Then let me show you," he said in a fierce whisper. His hand slid inside the bodice of her dress. "Is it this?" Her breath caught as his fingers moved against the rise of her breasts. "Or this?" She fell back against the wall as he lifted her skirt. His fingers brushed the soft, inner flesh of her thighs, then traced the lace trim on her panties and slid beneath them.

A long, drawn out breath escaped her lungs. "Oh," she whispered, "oh . . ."

She lifted her head blindly and kissed him, her hands clasping the back of his head. She held nothing back, not her passion, not her need, not her desire.

"Oh, please," she whispered, "please, please, please..."

He laughed in triumph. "Yes," he said, "that is right, *bellissima*. Beg me. I want to hear you plead for my touch, for my possession."

That was what she wanted; *he* was what she wanted. From the beginning, from that electrifying moment when she'd felt him watching her at the Fabbiano showing, she'd wanted his kisses, wanted the thrust of his body into hers. She had done everything to deny the truth, but how could she deny it now, when she was burning under his touch?

Nicolo moved against her. She felt his heat, his hardness, and her bones turned to liquid. She knew that if he took her now, against this wall, she would not stop him.

She lifted herself, caught his face in her hands. "Nico..."

"Yes," he whispered fiercely, "oh, yes." His arms tightened around her and he laughed softly. "I knew I was right. You are not made of ice. You burn like a flame."

It was as if the windows had flown open and all the winds of winter had suddenly come sweeping into the room. She went still in his arms.

Of course. That was what this was all about. It was what the entire day had been about. His charm, his little anecdotes, even this scene played in the velvet darkness—all of it had been to answer the challenge she'd so foolishly set before him.

"I'm impervious to your charm," she'd said—and he, the great Prince Sabatini had had no choice but to prove her wrong.

Caroline shuddered with revulsion. The light switch. Dammit, it was here somewhere... Yes! Her hand closed on it, and light flooded the room.

Nicolo blinked in the sudden glare. *"Cara?"*

"Don't *'cara'* me, you—you..." Her hands balled into fists. "Get out of here!"

"Caroline." He was staring at her, confusion in his eyes. "What is it?"

"Get out or so help me, I'll yell so loud that I'll wake the whole house! I'll wake your ancestors! I'll wake half of Rome!"

Nicolo's smile faded, became a snarl of rage. His hands tightened on her until she thought she would cry out. But she wouldn't give him that satisfaction. Instead, she stood facing him, her head flung back, her eyes steady on his.

"Women like you play a dangerous game, *cara.*"

"You don't know a damned thing about women like me!"

"You are the same as Arianna," he growled. "That's all I have to know!"

He turned, pulled open the door, and vanished into the darkness.

CHAPTER NINE

CAROLINE PACED her bedroom, her furious steps taking her from one end of the handsome room to the other. Back and forth, back and forth she walked, like a caged tigress.

It was early morning; the sun was streaming in the windows and below, in the garden, a bird sang a happy greeting to the day, but Caroline was oblivious to it. All she could think about was what had happened in this room last night—what had almost happened, what, undoubtedly, *would* have happened—if Nicolo hadn't made the mistake of revealing his true intentions.

The smug, insolent bastard! If he'd been able to keep from gloating, she'd have ended up in his bed, which was what he'd intended right from the beginning.

Caroline's mouth twisted. Instead, she'd become a member of what had to be a rather exclusive club.

"You are the same as Arianna," he'd said with disgust, but it was actually a compliment! Apparently, she and Arianna were members—for all she knew, the *only* members—of the "I Refused to Sleep with Nicolo Sabatini Sorority."

Whatever else the mysterious Arianna might be, she was clearly a woman of taste.

Caroline strode to the windows and plumped her hands down on the sill. She had never been this angry in her life. Never, not even when some aroused, overweight, ugly Casanova had tried to paw her. At least men like that had been upfront about what they wanted, they hadn't schemed and plotted with Machiavellian determination.

But that was what Nicolo had done. That was what yesterday afternoon and evening had been all about. The little jokes, the smiles, the anecdotes about his childhood, about his city, had been nothing but clever prelude to her seduction but the worst of it was that she'd been so damnably easy to seduce. She'd made an absolute fool of herself. Nothing, *nothing*, could compensate for that.

Caroline sank down on to the edge of the bed and shut her eyes tightly, trying to block out the humiliating scene, but it was impossible. Her whispers of abandonment seemed to echo in the air of the bedroom.

"Nico," she could hear herself saying, *"Nico, please, please, please..."*

A shudder went through her. She'd behaved like a wanton, and why? She'd always known what he was, and she— she was no silly eighteen-year-old who'd never known a man's touch. She was a woman, and, even if she was hardly the sophisticate Nicolo imagined her to be, at least she knew what passion was.

She rose and stalked across the room, snatched her brush from the vanity table and dragged it through her hair with harsh, angry strokes. But she was vulnerable, and the great Prince Sabatini knew it. She was in a strange country, with no friends, no family, and only the barest grasp of the language...

"Damn the man!" Caroline whispered fiercely as she dropped the brush to the top of the vanity unit.

Caroline looked into the mirror and her grim reflection looked back at her. How she hated him! She was already counting the minutes until she'd march out the front door of the Palazzo Sabatini, secure in the knowledge that she'd never again have to see that self-satisfied patrician face. If it hadn't been for Anna, she'd have been gone at sunrise.

But she couldn't just walk out of the old woman's life, not without preparing her first. An explanation was easy enough.

"I'm homesick for the States, Anna," she'd say.

And then, in a day or two, she'd say the homesickness was getting worse, that she was terribly sorry but she was going to have to leave Rome.

She owed the Princess that much. Hell, it wasn't *her* fault she had a scoundrel for a grandson.

As for Nicolo—Caroline grimaced. "The *palazzo* was enormous; they could avoid each other easily, and, unless she was altogether crazy, he'd be as happy about that as she was.

Caroline took another look at the mirror. "All you have to do is hang in for a couple of days," she told herself.

And if Nicolo tried to make an issue of the fact that he'd bought out her contract so she could work for him, he could stuff it!

To hell with him, and the contract, both. Just another couple of days, and it would be, *"Arrivederci, Roma!"*

HE WAS ALREADY GONE when she came down to breakfast, which didn't surprise her at all. Anna chattered on and on, explaining that Nicolo had been called away early on business.

"Did you enjoy yourself yesterday, my dear?" she asked.

"Oh, yes," Caroline said, but as soon as she could, she changed the subject.

It was midmorning when Nicolo called. Lucia brought Anna the phone.

"Nicolo," Anna said happily, *"che cosa fa?"*

Caroline closed her ears to the conversation, not that she could understand the swift, musical Italian. It was time to begin hinting at her departure; she'd put it off as long as she could, but it had to be done.

"Anna," she said, after the phone call ended, "I've been thinking..."

"Yes, dear? What is it?"

Caroline ran the tip of her tongue across her lips.

"It's just that—well, I'm so happy you're feeling better."

"Oh, I certainly am!" Anna beamed. "Thanks to you."

Caroline shook her head. "I think you ought to give credit to your doctors," she said gently. "And to yourself."

The Princess frowned. "What is it, Caroline? You look so sad."

"Well, I—I'm feeling a bit sad, actually." She took a breath. "I suppose I'm homesick."

"Then my news could not have come at a better time!"
The old woman smiled happily. "Nicolo is bringing guests
for dinner. Business acquaintances, you would call them, the
ones with whom he spent last week."

"I'm sure that will be lovely for you, Anna."

"We have not had a dinner party in this house for such a
long time! I know some of the guests who will be here, Caroline, the ones who work for Nico. Signor Tomba and his
wife, and the Spinellis, and the Valentis and their charming
daughter..." Anna smiled and reached for Caroline's hand.
"But the best news is that one of the guests is an American!
Someone from your very own country, my dear. That
should help your mood!"

Caroline shook her head. "I really don't think so," she
said quickly. "I—er—I feel under the weather today. I'd just
as soon have my dinner in my room."

"Nonsense," Anna said briskly. "An evening like this is
just what you need."

"Anna..."

The Princess's hand tightened on Caroline's. "Oh, please,
my dear, don't disappoint me! I could never enjoy myself,
knowing you were in your room alone."

Caroline stared at Anna. An evening spent in the company of Nicolo Sabatini? A sentence to purgatory would
have sounded more enticing, but then, this would be her last
evening in the *palazzo*.

"In that case," she said with a little smile, "how could I
turn down your kind invitation?"

Anna beamed happily. "Good, good. Now let me see...
What sort of meal shall I ask Cook to prepare?"

BY EIGHT, Caroline was filled with misgivings. She should
never have allowed her wish to please Anna to influence her,
she thought as she slipped on a pair of delicate, high-heeled
black silk pumps. She'd sworn she'd never spend another
moment in Nicolo's company and now here she was, about
to endure who knew how many hours of it.

Caroline straightened and walked to the mirror. Well, it
was too late to back out now. She'd just have to grit her
teeth and survive the evening. At least, Anna would have

this party to remember tomorrow, when Caroline announced she was leaving. Perhaps it would make things easier.

She gave herself a critical glance, taking in the ankle-length, black lace gown with its full skirt, long, tapered sleeves and off-the-shoulder neckline. It was the perfect foil for her coloring; she looked cool and composed and that was how she would behave tonight, despite the fact that even the thought of having to spend an evening in Nicolo's company made her stomach clench.

Carefully, she drew her hair back from her temples, securing it with a pair of jet clips that had been her grandmother's. She screwed a pair of gold hoops into her earlobes, moistened her lips and pasted on the impersonal smile that had served her so well during her months on the catwalk.

The stairway was deserted. When she reached the atrium, she could hear the faint hum of voices and laughter coming from the library, where drinks were being served beside the fire—for the weather had reverted to normal, and there was a chill in the air this evening.

"There you are, dear," Anna said as Caroline stepped into the room.

"We were just talking about you."

Faces turned in her direction, and Caroline smiled politely.

"I'm sorry I'm late, Anna."

"You're not late at all, and, even if you were, you were worth waiting for. You look lovely." Anna smiled as she took her hand and tucked it into hers. "Let me introduce you to some of the other guests."

There were too many names to remember, especially when she was so tense. She looked around the room for Nicolo. Where was he? It was uncomfortable enough, knowing she would have to face him, but it was worse not to know when, to wonder if she would turn around suddenly and find him watching her with those cold, cold eyes . . ."

"The Valentis," Anna said with a smile, "and their charming daughter, Sofia."

Caroline forced her attention to the middle-aged couple, who smiled and greeted her in almost flawless English. Sofia, a beautiful, dark-eyed girl of perhaps eighteen, smiled shyly and whispered a breathy *"Buona sera."*

"And last but certainly not least, your countryman, Mr. Robert Calder."

Calder was a tall, rangy man in his thirties with an open grin and a Midwestern twang.

"Hi there," he said, taking Caroline's hand.

"I leave you in Mr. Calder's good hands," Anna said, and the American's smile became a grin.

"Good thinking, Princess," he said, with an easy charm that made up for any lack of etiquette. "Well, well, Miss Bishop. I never dreamed I'd find an American beauty in the heart of Rome."

She smiled. "What brings you to Italy, Mr. Calder?"

"Call me Bob, please. My firm's been seeking the backing of the Prince's financial group," he said, nodding toward the far side of the room, "and—"

But Caroline had stopped listening. Nicolo was there, standing just where Bob Calder had indicated, the only person who had not in any way acknowledged her presence. He was dressed formally, in a dark dinner suit that emphasized the width of his shoulders and the whipcord hardness of his body, his dark Roman head inclined slightly toward the woman standing beside him.

Something twisted deep inside her heart. Nicolo, she thought, oh, Nicolo..."

He turned and looked at her, as if in answer. For a tick of eternity, his sapphire eyes seemed to burn through her, and then he said something to the woman, touched her lightly on the arm, and started across the room.

She took an instinctive step back and brushed against a small marble horse that stood on a pedestal.

"Whoops." Bob Calder grinned and put a steadying hand on her arm just as Nicolo reached them.

"Caroline." His gaze went to Calder's hand, then to her face. "I see you have met Mr. Calder."

"She sure has, Your Highness." Calder chuckled. "I warn you, I'm going to monopolize this young lady all evening."

She saw Nicolo's jaw tighten. "Is that right?" he said evenly.

"We've got lots to talk about, haven't we, Caro?" He grinned. "You don't mind if I call you Caro, do you?"

"Please do," she said. "It's what everyone calls me back home."

What was the matter with her? No one called her that; she was Caroline, she always had been. She'd always liked the plain, old-fashioned simplicity of the name. And why was she letting Bob Calder clamp his hand on her arm this way?

"How nice," Nicolo said. His voice had grown even colder, but Calder didn't seem to notice. He gave Caroline a quick, mirthless smile. "Anna was right when she said you should be asked to attend our little gathering."

Caroline's eyes narrowed. So. He had not wanted her to be here any more than she'd wanted to come.

She managed to smile politely. "I'm beginning to be glad I let her talk me into coming."

Nicolo's jaw tightened, and she knew the barb had found its mark.

"I should like to see you alone for a moment, Caroline, if you please."

Caroline looked at Bob Calder, "You don't mind, do you?" she asked sweetly, but, before he could answer, Nicolo grasped her arm and took her aside.

"What kind of nonsense is this?" he demanded in a low growl.

"Nonsense? What do you mean, nonsense?" Caroline twisted a little against his hand. "Be careful, Your Highness, or you're liable to make a spectacle of yourself."

"Perhaps you've forgotten, Caroline—such things don't mean a thing to me."

"Not even in your own home?" They reached an unoccupied corner of the room. Nicolo swung her toward him and his hand dropped to his side.

"Why did you accept *la Principessa*'s invitation?" His eyes glittered with anger. "Surely you knew it was not my wish to have you here this evening?"

"It was not my wish to be here at all, starting with day one!" Caroline glared back at him. "But you can stop worrying. I'm leaving tomorrow."

"Leaving?" His lips drew back from his teeth. "That is more nonsense! You will not leave here until I give you permission."

Caroline's eyes widened. "Permission? *Permission?* I hate to burst your royal bubble, Excellency, but I'm free to come and go as I please."

"You forget yourself," he said in a low, threatening voice. "You are in my home, *cara*. I make the rules here, no one else. You will leave when I say you may, not a moment sooner!"

"Nico?" Anna Sabatini stepped between them, a fixed smile on her face. "Nico, Monsieur Beauchamp has arrived." She looked from her grandson's angry glower to Caroline's pale face. "Whatever is the matter with you two?"

Nicolo blew out his breath. "Nothing, *carissima*," he said. He smiled, took his grandmother's hand, and pressed his lips to it. "Caroline and I were simply arguing over an appropriate bedtime for you."

Anna laughed, "I have solved the problem, then. I shall go up when we finish coffee. Now, go, Nico, greet your guest." She linked her arm through Caroline's. "I will take care of Caroline."

But it was Bob Calder who assumed that role. He brought her a drink, offered her a cigarette. He was charming and witty, but, although Caroline was polite, she offered no encouragement. In fact, it was hard for her to keep up her end of the conversation. She couldn't stop thinking about Nicolo, about how he'd treated her, not just last night but moments before. What kind of man was he, anyway?

It was obvious what kind of man Sofia Valenti thought he was. The girl's every smile, every glance, was filled with adoration that grew more and more obvious as the evening went on and as her consumption of champagne increased.

She hung on his every word at dinner, and after coffee, when *la Principessa* excused herself and retired and the little group adjourned to the living room for liqueurs and brandy, Sofia dropped to a cushion at his feet and gazed worshipfully into his face.

"Just look at that child make calf eyes at the Prince," Calder said with a soft chuckle.

Nicolo was the only one who seemed unaware of the girl's fawning attention, which was too bad, Caroline thought grimly. A child like that was probably just what he needed. Young. Innocent. Malleable. Just the type of blank page made to suit a man like him.

Caroline put down her coffee. "Excuse me," she said to Calder, and she made her way from the living room to the elegant powder room down the hall.

Once inside, she sank onto the quilted bench opposite the marble vanity and stared at her reflection. This was ridiculous. What was there to be upset about? She'd worried that seeing Nicolo tonight would make her feel uncomfortable, but it hadn't, except for that first unpleasant encounter. And by this time tomorrow—

There was a soft rap at the door.

"Yes?" Caroline said.

Sofia Valenti stepped into the room.

"I hope I am not imposing, *signorina*."

"Not at all. I was just leaving."

The girl's tongue snaked along her full lips. "I wonder—have you a moment?"

Caroline looked at her. "Of course. What is it?"

Sofia swallowed hard. "This is so—how do you say?—it is not easy for me to say, *signorina*."

"I'm afraid I don't understand."

Sofia hesitated. Caroline could almost see her building up her courage, and then her words came out in a rush.

"I want you to know I am not jealous of your presence in the *palazzo*," she said.

Caroline's brows lifted. "Why should you be?"

"I—I mean, I know you are beautiful. A woman of the world, and much older..."

Caroline laughed. "Such compliments, Sofia. I'm not sure I'm up to them."

The girl sank down beside her. "But you are not His Excellency's sort at all," she said seriously. "I understand that."

Caroline's smile fled. "There's no reason I should be," she said coldly. "I'm here to provide companionship for Princess Sabatini, not for him."

Sofia put her hand on Caroline's arm. "I am making a mess of this," she said quickly. "What I meant to say is, I do not feel any animosity to you, *signorina*."

"Well good for you! Now, if you'll excuse me . . ."

"I suppose you are aware that the Prince is very old-fashioned."

"If you mean the Prince thinks we'd be better off if the clock were set back a couple of hundred years," Caroline said, "the answer is yes."

"My father, as well, believes in the old ways." Sofia's eyes met Caroline's. "As, *per esempio*, in arranged marriages."

"Well, I still don't . . ." Caroline's mouth dropped open. "Marriage? Yours—and Prince Sabatini's?"

"Oh, please, you must not say a word to anyone!" The girl gave a worried glance over her shoulder, as if she might find the dinner guests all crowded inside the room with them. "The arrangements are not yet concluded, you see, and— Why do you look at me that way, *signorina*? Such betrothals are not so uncommon, even today, in our world."

Nicolo and this child were to marry! And he'd known it, all the time he'd been trying to bed her.

"Have I upset you?" the girl said in a worried tone.

Caroline took a deep breath. "No," she said calmly, "not at all. I just don't understand why you've taken me into your confidence."

"I thought—I hoped—you might be able to help me. A woman like you—you must know ways to get a man to . . ." she flushed ". . . to want someone."

"Me?" Caroline didn't know if she wanted to laugh or to cry. "You want me to help you seduce Nicolo?"

Sofia's face flamed. "He—he treats me like a child. He is very kind, even gallant, but he never—when he looks at me..." She swallowed. "If you could, perhaps, make some suggestions, you see, so that I might move things along...?"

Caroline felt a stir of anger deep within her breast, not at this artless, naive girl but at Nicolo, Nicolo with his phony morality, his counterfeit Old World manners—his way of finding a woman's heart and using it to suit his own needs, whether she was eighteen or twenty-four or seventy...

"I should not have asked," the girl said unhappily. "Forgive me—"

Caroline stood up. "When we go back inside," she said tightly, "keep your eye on me and Mr. Calder." She forced herself to smile. "I'm sure you'll be able to pick up some ideas."

She pulled open the bathroom door and hurried through the atrium, her heels tapping swiftly against the mosaic floor. Someone had put on the stereo and music drifted from the living room. Outside the doorway, she paused, took a deep breath, and made the sort of entrance she'd sworn she'd never make again, her stride long and sensual, her head back so that her hair moved against her bare shoulders, her mouth curved into a soft, sexy smile.

Nicolo was standing on the far side of the room, talking with Bob Calder.

"Bob," she said brightly, in a tone she knew would draw the attention of everyone. She held out her arms as both men turned and looked at her. She saw Nicolo's eyes narrow to slits, and then Calder was moving past him, hands outstretched to clasp hers.

"There you are, Bob. I was afraid, for a moment, that I'd lost you."

Calder grinned as their fingers interlaced. "You're not likely to do that, Caro."

"Good." Her smile grew brilliant. "I'd hate to lose you so soon after I've found you."

A delighted flush rose on Calder's cheeks. He put his arm around her waist and smiled at her and she thought, with a sharp twinge of guilt, that he was much too nice a man to use this way.

But just then she looked up and saw Nicolo watching them, his face as black as a storm cloud, and her chin lifted.

That's right, Prince, she thought coldly. Look. That's the only thing you'll ever do. You'll look—but you won't touch, ever again.

She smiled and leaned closer to Calder, so that the bright fall of her golden hair brushed his jaw.

"Tell me about yourself," she said.

He did, for what seemed like the next million hours. And Caroline, who had never developed the art of flirting, behaved as if it came as naturally to her as breathing. She batted her lashes, laughed at Calder's jokes, found reasons to touch him.

She saw Nicolo watching them out of the corner of her eye.

That's right, she thought, while she smiled at yet another of Calder's stories. Suffer, you bastard... Watch me and wonder what would have happened if I hadn't sent you away last night, if I'd done what I longed to do, if I'd let you make love to me...

She made a little sound of distress, and Calder stopped in the midst of his story.

"Caro? Is something the matter?"

"No," she said quickly, "no, not at all. I was just thinking—I was thinking it's a waste, all that pretty music playing in the background and no one dancing."

Calder didn't hesitate. He took her hand and led her into the atrium, where she turned and went into his arms. He held her close, both his arms around her waist, and she tucked her head under his chin. They swayed in time to the music, and then Calder cleared his throat.

"Caro? I was thinking. When the party ends, how'd you like to go someplace for a drink? I'm staying at the Hilton, and—"

"What an excellent suggestion, Signor Calder." Nicolo's voice was cold as the thrust of a knife; it drove them apart and they stood staring at him. "But I am afraid Caroline has other obligations when the party ends." His lips turned up in a terrible parody of a smile. "Isn't that right, *cara*?"

He reached out and looped his arm around her waist, his fingers splayed just beneath her breast. It was a lazy, almost careless gesture; only Caroline knew that the pressure of his hand was remorseless and proprietorial. She had little choice but to let him draw her close against him, until she was pressed tightly into the hard curve of his body.

"Nicolo, don't!"

"It is all right, *cara*, Signor Calder will understand." He touched his mouth to her hair in a way that was clearly possessive. "Caroline and I had a little quarrel last evening, *signore*." He shrugged and gave a little laugh. "You know how it can be, yes? Sometimes a man and his woman say things they should not..."

"That's not true! You and I—"

"I must accept some of the blame, I am afraid," he said with a smile that was clearly meant to signify one man would understand the foibles of another. "I made matters worse by—how do you say it?—not kissing and making up before bedtime."

Calder's face was turning an incredible shade of pink—but it could not be any pinker than her own face! Caroline shook her head and gave Calder a beseeching look.

"He didn't! I mean, we didn't! Bob, listen to me—"

"I have already admitted it, *bellissima*." Nicolo sighed. "I didn't. At the very least, I should have sent you flowers today, some trinket to prove my affection..." He laughed softly. "And so, she repaid me by paying a great deal of attention to you tonight, *signore*. Well, we both know how women are, eh?"

Caroline stamped her foot. "Damn you, Nicolo! Not a word of this is true. You're lying! Bob, I swear. He's lying..."

"Lying? Nicolo Sabatini, lie?" His dark brows drew together. "Would you call me a liar, Signor Calder?"

Calder shook his head dumbly.

"Indeed." Nicolo blew out his breath. "I am a patient man, *signore*. I understand you were an innocent dupe in Caroline's little game, but I assure you, I will not tolerate being called a liar."

"I—I'd never call you that, Your Highness." Calder's Adam's apple bobbed as he swallowed. "And—and I'm sorry if there was any misunderstanding about—about—"

"I accept your apology," Nicolo said graciously.

"Wait a minute!" Caroline's voice rose alarmingly. "Wait just a damned minute..."

"It is late," he said with a gentle smile. "I think I must say good-night to my guests, yes?" He spun her to him, then gave her a swift, hard kiss on her mouth. "You go on up, *cara*," he said softly. "Make yourself even more beautiful for me. That white silk *peignoir* set, yes? The one I gave you last week? And I will make your apologies for you." Smiling, he patted her backside, then pushed her gently toward the stairs.

Caroline stared at him, stunned, hating him with such blinding rage that she didn't trust herself to speak. At last, she swung toward Bob Calder, but he averted his eyes.

"Nicolo," she sputtered, "you—you—"

"She is a tigress," he said to Calder, who smiled in nervous agreement. "Go on, *cara*. I promise, I will not keep you waiting long."

She wanted to shriek, to curse him into all eternity—but he had already turned his back and was strolling toward the living room.

The last thing she saw, before she turned and flew up the stairs, was the embarrassment on Bob Calder's face—and the shock on the face of Sofia Valenti, who stood huddled in a shadowed corner.

CHAPTER TEN

CAROLINE FLUNG open her bedroom door, then slammed it shut after her. That son of a bitch! That sewer rat! That no-account, blue-blooded bastard...

Her shoes went flying as she kicked them off her feet.

"I hate you, Nicolo Sabatini," she said.

Her skirt swirled around her legs in a froth of black lace as she stalked across the room.

"Do you hear me? I *hate* you!"

Of course he couldn't hear her. He was still downstairs, playing the charming host.

"Some charm," she muttered as she threw herself down on the bed. If only those people knew what she knew...

Not that it would mean a damn. Nicolo could get away with anything, it seemed. Bob Calder, that ass, was more than willing to accept him as a man who knew all there was to know about women. Signor Valenti was willing to accept him as a son-in-law. And Sofia, that foolish child, was eager to accept him any way she could get him!

Caroline sat up. Poor Sofia. She'd looked as if she'd seen the devil himself. Well, maybe it was for the best. Maybe it would change her mind about the great Prince Sabatini, maybe she'd ask her papa to marry her off to someone who believed in a woman's right to decency and respect.

Caroline got to her feet. Her anger last night had been nothing compared to this. How dared Nicolo treat her this way? He had forced his way into her life, arranged things so that she'd had no choice but to do his bidding—and as soon as she'd done something to make it clear that she was still her own person and not his, he'd humiliated her.

Of course, that wasn't how he'd see it. As far as Nicolo was concerned, *he* was the injured party. She'd dented that enormous ego of his, hadn't she?

Why had she even wasted time trying to defend herself? It didn't matter a damn to her what Bob Calder thought of her. What counted was what she thought of herself. She had integrity. She had convictions. And Nicolo had trampled on all of them from day one, and she was damned well going to tell that to him tomorrow morning, after she said good-bye to Anna and...

"No!"

She spat the word into the silence. No, to hell with waiting until tomorrow to deliver her message to the bastard, she thought grimly as she marched to the door and yanked it open. He would hear what she had to say now. Tonight. And if he threw her out of the *palazzo* afterward, so what? Maybe it was time Anna faced reality and dealt with the truth about her beloved grandson.

She flew down the stairs and across the atrium floor, her heels clicking against the tiles.

"Nicolo!" she said, flinging open the library door—but the room was empty. The living room, then; he would be having a last brandy in the living room—

No. It was empty, too, and the garden was dark.

She glanced up the wide staircase. There was only one other place he could be: in his private apartments on the third floor. Caroline gathered her skirt in her hand and hurried up the steps.

A dim night-light cast her shadow against the closed double doors she knew opened on to his rooms. She strode toward them, her fist upraised—but just before she pounded on it, she hesitated.

Maybe—maybe she ought to wait until morning to confront him. He'd been so angry; she had never seen him quite that way before.

Wait? How could she wait? How could she permit another minute to pass without telling him, to his face, what he could do with his lies and insinuations?

Caroline lifted her hand and rapped her knuckles sharply against the door. The sound, loud and sharp as a gunshot, faded into the silence. She rapped again, harder than before.

"Nicolo!" she said furiously, "open the door!"

More silence.

"Dammit," she snapped, and she pounded on the door with both hands. "Do you hear me, Nicolo? I want to—"

The doors swung open, and Caroline almost fell into the room. Nicolo stood before her, wearing his pants and nothing else, a cold smile on his face.

"Caro," he said politely as he shut the door after her. "What a charming surprise."

"I want to talk to you," she snapped.

"Of course, Caro."

"Don't call me that!"

"No?" He lifted one tanned shoulder in a lazy shrug. "Ah. My mistake. I simply assumed you would much prefer that charming nickname to your own. Isn't that what you told your friend, Mr. Calder?"

"He is not my friend. And I do not care to be called that." She looked at him. "Not—not the way you say it."

"Ah. I understand. You prefer the name spoken with an American accent. Of course."

Caroline glared at him. "Will you stop that?"

"What?"

"That," she said, throwing out her hand. "That—that smarmy tone of voice."

Nicolo frowned. "What does this mean, 'smarmy'?"

"It means—it means . . ." She looked at him, then blew out her breath. "Never mind what it means. I told you, I want to talk to you."

His eyes narrowed. "And it could not wait until morning?"

"That's right. It couldn't."

He folded his arms across his bare chest, the disdainful smile replaced by a stern, fixed stare.

"Then talk."

Caroline stared at him. It had never occurred to her that he'd have been on his way to bed. But he must have been; that was why he was shirtless. It was why his bare toes peeped out from beneath his pants, why the pants themselves were unsnapped at the waist so they rode low on his hips, why the beautiful musculature of his powerful shoulders and arms was so visible...

She looked away. "I can wait until you've put on a shirt," she said stiffly.

"Then you'll wait until tomorrow, *cara*," he snapped, "for I've no intention of getting dressed again until then. Now either make your little speech or—"

"Little speech?" She swung around and faced him, her hands on her hips. "Little speech? Children and fools make 'little speeches,' Nicolo, and by God, I am neither."

He gave her a cold smile. "Not a child, *cara*. No, you are certainly not that. As for the other—"

"That's what you tried your damnedest to do tonight, wasn't it? Make me look like—like an idiot! But—"

Nicolo laughed. "I cannot accept credit where none is due." He leaned back against the door and stuffed his hands into his pockets. "You may take all the credit for that, Caroline."

She looked at him again. What did it matter if the change in posture meant she could see all of his chest now, the hard planes, the well-defined muscles? What did it matter if the way he was standing, with his hands in his pockets, tightened the fine wool of his pants across his loins and thighs?

"Caroline?" Her eyes flew to his face. "For a woman who wished to talk, you are surprisingly silent."

Damn him anyway! Was he laughing at her? Caroline's spine stiffened.

"I am not in the habit of holding discussions with half-naked men," she said coldly. "Surely it isn't asking too much of you to put some clothes on, Your Highness."

His brows rose. After a moment, he shrugged his shoulders.

"If it pleases you," he said.

She nodded curtly as he padded toward a door on the far wall. Caroline let out her breath once he was gone. Anyone would have felt at a disadvantage in such a situation. She had come here to confront him, not to—to be forced to endure the sight of his nudity...

But he hadn't been nude. Not really. If he had, she'd have seen those long legs, whose stride outmatched even hers, she'd have seen the power of his masculinity...

She gave herself a brisk shake. What the hell was the matter with her? She felt amazingly disoriented, but why? She'd had little to drink tonight, perhaps two glasses of champagne all evening. Perhaps this was the result of an adrenalin rush from all that anger.

Yes. That was exactly what it was. She had just a minute or two to collect herself before Nicolo returned. You couldn't beard the lion in his den if you let your fears get the best of you.

She wrapped her arms around herself and began to pace the room. Concentrate on something outside yourself, she thought. Concentrate on—on this room.

It was a large room, softly illuminated by the light cast by a handsome brass *torchère* in the far corner. The carpet beneath her feet was, she thought, an antique Persian, its deep blues and maroons softened and made even lovelier by decades of use. There was a marble fireplace opposite the door; she walked slowly to it and ran her hand lightly over the back of one of the small, velvet-covered sofas that flanked it. A small table stood nearby on which ivory chessmen stood poised in combat on an inlaid board.

The room surprised her a little. It was as filled with rare and handsome things as any other in the *palazzo*, yet it had a different feel to it, as if its owner had furnished it more with an eye to what pleased him than to effect.

"If you have finished touring my sitting room, perhaps we can get on with this."

Caroline spun around. Nicolo was standing in the center of the room, scowling darkly at her. Her gaze flew over him. He was still barefoot, but he had put on a shirt. But he hadn't closed it; it hung open, revealing his shadowed torso.

Caroline lifted her chin. "I suppose you think I came here demanding an apology," she said coldly.

"I hope not. If you did, you're wasting your time."

She flushed. This wasn't going the way she'd intended. Sometime between knocking on Nicolo's door and stepping inside his apartment, she'd lost the advantage her anger had provided. Soon, if she wasn't careful, she'd be just where she knew he wanted her. On the defensive.

"Just what did you think you were doing down there?" she demanded, putting her hands on her hips.

Nicolo walked to a cabinet with Murano glass doors. "Do you mean, after you made your somewhat hasty departure?" He pulled open a door and took out a decanter and a balloon snifter. "Well, first I assured your Signor Calder that his company was not about to lose Sabatini's financial backing—"

"*My* Calder? He was your guest, not mine."

"What happened was surely not his fault," he said, continuing as if she hadn't spoken. He uncorked the decanter and poured a dollop of golden brandy into the snifter. "Then I said good-night to my guests." He gave her a cool smile over the rim of the snifter. "You remember them, don't you, *cara*? Those people who innocently came to my house this evening, expecting a pleasant dinner, good wine, enjoyable conversation—and instead were treated to a vulgar display?"

"The only vulgar display that took place tonight was yours," Caroline snapped. "You have one hell of a nerve, making me look—"

"I have asked you repeatedly not to be crude in my presence!"

"Ask? Ask?" Caroline strode forward, her hands on her hips. "You have never asked me anything, Your Royal Imperialness! In fact, I'd bet you've never asked *anyone* anything in your whole life! What you do is demand. You order. You—you—"

"No wonder there is no man in your life," he said, slamming the snifter down on a tabletop. "Who could tolerate you?"

"It's not a question of tolerance, but one of respect!" She glared at him. "Maybe some Italian women will put up with being treated as if they are children, but American women—"

"Please!" Nicolo threw up his hands. "I have learned all I wish to know of American women. You're right—I don't

understand them. But I have never shown a woman anything but respect."

"How can you say that? This evening, you treated me
like—like—"

"Like what?" he demanded. "Would you prefer that I do
what some man should have done years ago? Should I have
turned you over my knee and spanked the daylights out of
you?"

"You see? You even talk to a woman as if she were a
child. But then, that's the sort of woman you prefer, isn't it?
One who's young and helpless and—"

"You're being ridiculous, *cara*."

Caroline stamped her foot against the floor. "Don't *cara*
me, dammit!"

"You are not to use that kind of language!"

"And *you* are not to call me *cara*. I am not your 'dear,'
and I resent—"

"I will call you whatever I wish." His mouth twisted. "In
the old days—"

"But this isn't the old days. Boy, I'll just bet you wish it
were! Is there a rack in the basement of this *palazzo*?
Shackles on the wall? A cage to lock me in?"

"Once upon a time," he said grimly, "a woman knew her
place in a man's house."

"Back to that again! You never miss the chance to remind me that I'm living under your roof, do you?"

"Yes? And how have I done this, Caroline? By taking you
out of Milano and the greasy hands of Arturo Silvio and his
compatriots? By giving you employment? By paying you a
decent wage?" His hands shot to and clasped her shoulders. "Tell me, how have I gone about reminding you of my
authority?"

"Let go of me, Nicolo!"

"I have treated you with respect," he thundered. "I have
treated you with kindness and courtesy. And how do you
repay me?" His brows knotted in anger. "By making a fool
of me in front of my friends and associates, by acting
cheap—"

"Where was all that kindness, courtesy, and respect when you tried to seduce me last night?" she demanded, glaring at him.

A taut smile curved across his mouth.

"You were not an unwilling participant, *cara*."

Caroline felt her cheeks pinken, but she refused to drop her gaze from his.

"You never think of anyone but yourself, do you?"

He laughed. "Is that a critique of my skills as a lover?"

"It's a comment on your behavior in general," she snapped. "When I think of that poor child—"

His brows lifted. "What poor child?"

"I don't know which is worse, that you don't give a damn about respecting your commitment to her, or that you didn't think it would matter to me that you were—were trying to lure me into bed while all the time, you knew that you and she—"

"*Santa Maria!* You jump from topic to topic, like a flea in a room filled with dogs! How is a man to know what you are talking about?"

"You know what I'm talking about," she said furiously. "That poor girl . . ."

"First she is a poor *child*. Then she is a poor *girl*. Before, she was young and helpless." Nicolo let go of her and threw up his hands. "And still I have no idea who it is we discuss."

"Sofia Valenti, that's who." Caroline shook her head in disbelief. "Don't you care that she adores you?"

A smile curled across his lips, masculine and just a little smug.

"*Sì.* I know." He shrugged his shoulders. "What can I do? She will outgrow it, but until then—"

"She certainly will outgrow it. Marriage to you will surely cure her of any last—"

"Marriage? To me?" Nicolo stared at her as if she'd gone mad. "That child?"

"I agree. She *is* a child, but then, neither you nor her father would let that stop you. In fact, that's probably what makes her so desirable, the fact that she's young enough to be molded into whatever you think she ought to be—"

"By the bones of St. Peter! What are you talking about, woman?"

"—and that she's about as strong-willed as a—a rabbit!"

Nicolo stared at her as she fought for self-control. She was angry, yes, but why was her voice shaking like this? Why was her pulse galloping, as if her heart were surely going to leap from her breast?

"Let me understand this," he said slowly. He walked to the table where he'd left his brandy snifter, lifted it, and drained it of liquid. "I am to marry Sofia so that I can bask in the glow of her—her kitten love—"

"Puppy love," Caroline said furiously.

"Once we are wed, I will whisper some magic incantation into her ear and turn this—this *bambina* into a woman who will eagerly obey my every command. Is that what you think?"

Caroline shrugged. "That sounds close enough."

Nicolo's mouth turned down. "And who gave you all this priceless information, *cara*?"

"You're breaking the girl's heart, Nicolo. She loves you, and—"

"She has a schoolgirl crush on me, for God's sake!" He slammed down the snifter again and flung his hands onto his hips. "Her father and I wait for the day she grows out of it, but—"

"Don't lie! You're going to marry her! She told me that you and Valenti have worked up an arrangement . . ."

She broke off in bewilderment. Nicolo had flung his head back; he was laughing as if she had just told the world's funniest joke.

"She told you? The girl tells you this—this fairy tale, and you believe it?" His laughter stopped as quickly as it had begun. "Show me some respect at least, *cara*," he snapped. "Do you really think a man like me would be interested in a child like that? Her father and I have talked, yes. We have discussed her infatuation, which we agreed we would best handle by ignoring it." His eyes turned as cold as his voice. "I assure you, Caroline, when I decide it is time to take a wife, I will choose the correct one for a man in my position."

Of course he would. She had never thought otherwise. Then, why did the blunt words hurt?

"What I fail to understand is why you should have been so distressed by Sofia's fantasy."

"I told you why. I thought—"

"You have already told me what you thought." He gave her a long, searching look, and slowly, the coldness in his face began to fade. "You thought I had tried to make love to you despite this supposed betrothal." He smiled. "And," he said, very softly, "you were offended."

"Of course. It wouldn't have been right if—"

"Why were you offended? Even if you think me the most immoral bastard ever to walk the face of the earth, why would you react so personally? And why would you have set out to humiliate me?" His hand curled around the nape of her neck, the pressure of it light but steady so that she had no choice but to lift her head and meet his gaze. "I find something—how do you say it?—I find something very much out of kilter here."

She wanted to look away, to look anywhere but into his eyes, but it was impossible.

"If you don't understand something as simple as—as morality," she said stiffly, "then—"

He smiled again and ran his knuckles lightly along her flushed cheek.

"You were jealous," he said softly.

"Jealous?" she said incredulously. "You have your English twisted again, Nicolo. I wasn't jealous. I was angry. There's a difference."

He gave her an amused smile. "Is there?"

He was standing very close to her now; she could smell the scent of him, see the tiny laugh lines that fanned out from his eyes. A lock of dark hair had fallen down over his forehead and she was swept by a sudden yearning to put up her hand, feel the silken texture of it with her fingers.

She turned away sharply, but he caught hold of her arm.

"Look at me, *cara*."

Caroline's heart clenched. "It's late. I only came here to—tell you I'm leaving in the morning."

Gently, he turned her to face him. Her head drooped, and he put a finger beneath her chin.

"*Cara. Mia bellissima.* Look at me, please."

"I told you, it's late. And—"

"I agree." His arms went around her; she wanted to push him away, but his skin, naked and warm beneath the open shirt, brushed hers and she felt suddenly boneless. "It is very late." He bent and touched his lips to her hair, to her temple, and she swayed a little in his arms. "I should have made love to you long before this."

His whispered words sent a wave of longing through her body. She shook her head in a desperate denial.

"How can you say that? I don't—"

"What? Don't want me?" He urged her face up, until their eyes met and he smiled, showing a glimpse of even, white teeth. "Very well, *cara*. Tell me so, and I will let you go."

"You think you're so clever. But I—I—"

Her breath caught as his lips brushed her ear.

"I dream of you, *cara*." He nuzzled the hair back from her throat and pressed his mouth to her skin. "Can you imagine? I have not had such dreams since I was a boy." She sighed and her head fell back as his lips found the pulse beat in the hollow of her throat. "Do you dream of me, even a little?"

Had she dreamed of him? She thought she might have, that he had come to her in her sleep, whispered to her as he was whispering to her now, but she had forced the dream images away, she had denied them as she had denied what he wanted of her from the beginning.

But how could she deny anything now, when she was in his arms? He had kissed her before and turned her to fire, but now—oh, now she was more than fire, she was a glowing rivulet of flame, pulsing with heat.

"Nicolo," she whispered.

The word sighed softly into the shadows of the room. Nicolo murmured something soft and passionate into her ear. Caroline didn't understand the words, but there was no need for words now. He had gathered her closer in his arms, he was holding her so tightly that she couldn't tell whose heartbeat it was she felt throbbing within her bones, his or hers.

"Say it." His hands cupped her face. "Look at me, and tell me what it is you want me to do, *cara*."

She looked up slowly, her gaze moving over his face. That arrogant face. And it was true. He was arrogant. He was demanding. He was the Old World and she was the New.

But oh, he had set her heart to racing the instant she'd first seen him. I don't want you, she'd said, and he had insisted the same. But it had been a lie. They had wanted each other from that first night, and now, in this dimly lit room, with Nicolo's mouth on hers, with his hands on her breasts, she had finally run out of lies and excuses, not just for him but for herself.

She smiled languorously as she put her arms around his neck.

"Nico," she whispered.

It was just that one word, but it was enough. He groaned, caught her hand in his and pressed his mouth to the palm.

"Carissima," he said in an urgent whisper, and then he swung her into his arms and his mouth dropped to hers, slanting across her lips with hot, savage passion that drove the last bit of rational thought from her mind.

A table lamp threw a pool of soft luminescence across his bed. He put her down gently in the circle of golden light, then shrugged his shirt from his shoulders.

"You're beautiful," she said softly, watching as the light played across his skin, turning the tanned flesh gold.

Nicolo smiled. "It is you who are beautiful, *bellissima mia*." Slowly, his eyes never leaving her face, he reached behind her and undid the closure of her gown. It fell away from her shoulders, a spill of black froth in her lap. Nicolo drew the gown from her, and a thrill of pleasure raced along her spine as his eyes dropped to her body and the wisps of lace that still covered her.

"Amore," he murmured. He stroked his hand lightly over her mouth. Her lips parted and she sucked on his forefin-

ger, and then he trailed it down her throat, to the shadowed cleft between her breasts.

A shudder went through her as he bent his head and kissed them, and when his teeth closed lightly over the sheer fabric, first on one nipple and then on the other, she cried out.

"Yes," she said, "oh, yes."

He undid the fastener that held her bra closed and slipped it from her arms, then bent and kissed her naked breasts, biting gently at the aroused pink nubs until Caroline arched against him. He drew back and gave her a smile that made her blood thicken.

"Does it please you when I kiss your breasts, *cara*?" he murmured.

Her lashes fell to her cheeks. "You know it does," she whispered.

"Look at me," he said, and she did, slowly opening her eyes until they were fixed on his face. "I want to see into your soul while I make love to you, *mia Carolina*. I want to see the passion in your beautiful eyes when I touch you like this..."

She cried out as he lifted her hips and slid her panties from her. His fingertips brushed the inner flesh of her thighs, and suddenly he bent his head and pressed kisses to that most sensitive of soft flesh.

"Cristo," he whispered, "ah, the scent of your skin, *cara*, the taste of it..."

Her arms went around him, and she held him tight. "Make love to me now, Nico," she begged. "Please. Don't wait. I need—I need—"

He growled something deep in his throat as he rose from the bed. His pants fell to the carpet, and then he was beside her again, his skin hot against hers as he kissed her and kissed her. He rose above her and looked at her, his gaze moving over her with slow, lingering care, tasting her parted lips, her upthrust breasts, her parted thighs. He caught her hands in his and drew them over her head so that she lay open and vulnerable to him.

His eyes met hers, and what she saw in those burning blue depths sent a wave of pure sensation racing through her.

It was conquest, male conquest, pure and unrepentant. But she didn't resent it; she welcomed it, understood it, longed for it to make her complete.

"My Caroline," he said fiercely, and, with a powerful thrust, he entered her.

A sob burst from her lips as the night exploded around her and in that one moment Caroline understood.

There was no conqueror and no conquered when there was love. And she loved him. Oh, God, how she loved him, with all her heart and soul. She had loved him forever, and she always would.

Nicolo cried out her name, then gathered her close and kissed her, holding her so tightly that she felt the thundering beat of his heart.

"You are everything," he whispered fiercely. "Do you hear me, *cara*? You are everything!"

But she wasn't. She was not everything.

How could she be, when she wasn't the woman he loved?

CHAPTER ELEVEN

NICOLO ROLLED to his side, still holding Caroline close, caressing her, his hand following the curve of her hip, the swell of her breast. He dropped light kisses against her hair and her flushed cheeks.

"Mia adorata," he said against her mouth. "How beautiful you are."

She sighed as he kissed her again. "That was—it was—"

"Yes. Oh, yes, *cara*. It was."

They lay that way for long moments, until the race of their hearts slowed, and then Nicolo brought her head to his shoulder.

"Now I know you are not a dream," he whispered. "You are real. And wonderful."

Caroline pressed her lips to his chest. "You're the one who's wonderful."

He laughed softly. "Shall we argue over who is the most wonderful?"

She smiled. It felt so right, lying here in his arms. It was as if she had been waiting all her life to find this man, this moment.

"Maybe we'd better agree it's an argument no one can win," she said.

Nicolo shifted his weight so that he lay above her. "You think not?"

She smiled up at him, while she ran her fingers lightly over his muscled shoulders and back. It was such a silly conversation, she thought happily, the sort only lovers could have.

"Is that a dare?"

He laughed, then kissed the tip of her nose. "Another American idiom, *cara*? What does it mean?"

"It means you've no way to prove me wrong, Nico. If say you're wonderful, and you say I'm wonderful, we're a a stalemate."

He stretched lazily, and she caught her breath as she fel the sudden hardening of his body against hers.

"I warn you, *cara*, there is only one way to settle this dis pute."

Caroline felt the sudden heat coursing through her blood She smiled and let her hands drift down his spine to hi buttocks.

"What way?" she whispered.

A long time later, they lay quietly in each other's arm again.

"My tigress," Nicolo murmured.

Caroline smiled into the darkness. "I think I won the ar gument," she whispered.

He laughed and drew her closer. "Go to sleep. And then when you've had a chance to recover from your victory we'll fight the battle again."

Within moments, his breathing had slowed.

"Nico?" she said softly.

His arms tightened around her, but he didn't stir. Sh smiled again, and turned her face into his shoulder, inhal ing his scent. It was almost impossible to think that a cou ple of hours ago she'd have climbed on the rostrum in the Forum and denounced Prince Nicolo Sabatini to all o Rome.

He's insolent and impossible, she'd have said. He's ar rogant and authoritarian. He's stubborn and willful and...

She smiled into the darkness and slid her hand across hi chest. And he was still all of those things. It was only tha now, having finally admitted that she loved him, that she' loved him almost from the moment they'd met, she was abl to admit that it was those very same qualities that made hin the man he was.

His arrogance made him virile and masculine, his stub bornness gave him the character to administer his centu ries-old responsibilities. And, if there were times thos qualities seemed exaggerated, she understood. The prou blood of generations of Romans pulsed in his veins, mak ing him not just an ordinary man but Prince Nicolo Sabatini.

What woman wouldn't fall in love with him? What woman wouldn't want him?

The answer came with unwanted swiftness. Arianna, a voice inside her whispered. He had wanted Arianna, but she hadn't wanted him.

Caroline shifted uneasily. Why was she thinking about Arianna at a time like this? She only wanted to think about Nicolo, about the way she felt lying here, in his arms.

A pink tinge colored her cheeks as she remembered the things he'd whispered to her while they'd made love. She had understood some of them; others had needed no translation. His caresses had urged her to a wild, uninhibited passion she'd never known she possessed—but it was the love she felt for him that had sent her into such a breathtaking completion.

And yet, there was a strange emptiness in her heart. She'd longed to hear him whisper that he loved her—but he hadn't.

Had he whispered it to Arianna? Caroline shut her eyes tightly, trying to block out the sudden image of Nicolo and a woman whose face she could not see. He was holding her, kissing her, touching her...

Her throat constricted with emotion. She sat up and swung her legs to the side of the bed. Nicolo muttered something in his sleep; his arm reached out, his hand closing possessively around her wrist. She held her breath, waiting, until the bite of his fingers lessened. Then she gathered up her scattered clothing and stole from the room.

She dressed swiftly, then slipped out the door from his apartment into the silence of the sleeping *palazzo* and tiptoed stealthily down the stairs. Safe in her own room, she collapsed wearily back against the door.

Making love with Nicolo, giving in to the desire that had overwhelmed her, had been a mistake. She should have left Rome as she'd planned, she should never have looked into her heart and discovered a truth that could destroy her. She'd fallen desperately in love with a man who wasn't in love with her, a man who'd wanted her because she reminded him of a woman he wanted and couldn't have.

It was as simple, and as painful, as that.

Caroline stepped from her shoes, then from her dress. She made her way across the room. There'd be no happy ending to this story of the handsome prince and the beautiful princess, she thought as she sank onto the bed. That only happened in fairy tales. This was Rome, where legends of ancient gods persisted. In those stories, the prince almost always turned out to be a god who sought earthly pleasure from his love only until he tired of her.

Caroline's throat tightened. How soon would it be until her Prince felt the same way? She sank back against the pillows and threw her arm across her eyes. She *had* to leave today. Nicolo would be furious; she didn't even want to think about the extent of his rage. But to stay, to lie in his arms and each time know that he was dreaming of another woman, would not just break her heart but shatter it.

She rolled onto her belly and clutched her pillow. Her hair fell across her face, and she thought she could detect the faint scent of Nicolo's cologne lingering on the golden strands. She drew a deep, shuddering breath.

Nicolo, she thought, my love...

Eventually, she slept.

WHEN CAROLINE awakened, the sun was streaming in through the windows. She glanced at the bedside clock. There was just time to shower and dress before Lucia arrived, smiling shyly as she delivered the first cup of coffee of the new day.

She padded into the bathroom and turned on the spray. She wanted to see Anna, make her goodbyes in privacy, before she had to confront Nicolo and the scene she was certain he'd cause.

She dressed quickly in a white canvas skirt and navy cotton T-shirt. Her gaze flew to the clock again. Should she pack now or after she'd faced Nicolo?

After. Definitely after. She was running out of time and courage as it was, she admitted as she leaned into the wardrobe, searching for a pair of navy espadrilles. If she delayed another moment—

A knock sounded at the door. *"Avanti"* she called over her shoulder. The door snicked open. *"Grazie, Lucia. Sul tavolo, per favore."*

Strong arms closed around her. "Nicolo?" she whispered. Her heart swelled as he turned her toward him. He was so handsome, and dressed as casually as she was, in trim-fitting chino pants and tweed jacket worn open over a cotton-knit shirt. She smiled a little. "I—I thought you were Lucia."

"Parli l'Italiano molto bene, cara."

Caroline shook her head. "Not really. I've just picked up some words and phrases."

"Ah." His expression turned serious, although there was a hint of laughter in his eyes. "It is a command of idioms that makes the difference. Shall I teach you some?"

"Nicolo." Her smile faded. "Nicolo, we have to talk."

"Sì. We will—once you've bid me a proper good morning, the sort a woman gives a man after she's spent the night in his arms." He gathered her closer. "Like this," he murmured.

He kissed her with a slow, all-consuming sweetness that she could not resist. Her hands stole up his chest, then to his shoulders, and finally she clasped them behind his neck and gave herself up to the pleasure of the kiss.

After a long while, he smiled against her mouth, then drew back just enough so he was looking into her eyes.

"Now. Is there a better way to say good morning in your language, *carissima*?"

Caroline shook her head, then rested her forehead against his chin. "No," she admitted. "I guess that way is pretty universal."

"Caroline." Nicolo put his hand under her chin and lifted her face to his. "Why did you leave me, *bellissima*? I thought I would awaken with you in my arms this morning."

She drew a breath. "I know." Her hands slid to his forearms, and she stepped out of his embrace. "That's what I want to talk to you about, Nicolo." She turned away and busied herself straightening the bed. "I've thought things over, and—and I decided it would be best if—"

His arms closed around her. "Lucia will do that."

"It only takes a minute. I—"

"Caroline." He drew her back against him and pressed a kiss to the top of her head. "You didn't want to risk meeting one of the servants in the hall as you returned to your room, yes?"

She hesitated. That had certainly been part of her reason for slipping away.

"Yes, but—"

"I should have thought of it." He sighed. "But I was selfish. I could think only of how badly I wanted to make love to you again, with the sunshine on your beautiful face." His breath ruffled her hair as he kissed her ear lobe. "I missed you," he said softly.

Caroline closed her eyes. Tell him you're leaving, she thought. Tell him now.

"I—I missed you, too," she murmured.

He slid his hands up her midriff and cupped her breasts lightly while he nuzzled her hair aside and kissed her throat.

"Now, I will have to wait until tonight to make you mine again." He turned her in his arms. "What shall I do to keep my mind off that thought while the day passes?" He put his hands into her hair, lifting it from her shoulders, letting it sift through his fingers. "It will be hours before we can be together again." He laughed and swooped her into his arms. "Unless I do this—"

"Nicolo! Put me down!"

"—and carry you off to my bed."

She had to laugh. "Straight past Lucia, and Signora Brescia, the cook, the housekeeper, the gardener—"

"And Anna." He grinned. "You're right—and that's why I've decided on a different plan, one that will keep us safely out of temptation's way."

There was only one plan that would do that, Caroline thought, and it was hers. But Nicolo's smile was infectious, the feel of his arms wonderful. What harm could it do to play this little game another few minutes?

"And what is that, Your Highness?" she asked, looping her arms around his neck.

"I thought I would show you some more of my Roma. Mine," he said, with all possible emphasis on the word, "not the one in the guidebooks. The fountains in the Piazza Navona, and then the Fontana di Trevi, and the Campo de'Fiori where we can buy what we'll need for our picnic—"

"A picnic? Here, in Rome?"

"It would be possible. We could picnic on the grounds of the Villa Borghese." He bent and kissed her mouth until her lips softened beneath his. "But I know a special place, in the *campagna*—in the country—where you will see vineyards and ancient castles and rolling hills, where we can drink wine that the gods would have kept for themselves if they could." He smiled. "How does that sound, *cara*?"

"Wonderful. But—"

"There is a place where we can watch the setting sun paint the Tolfa Hills with scarlet. Then we'll drive back to the city and dine in a little *ristorante* in Trastevere where you'll eat the best *carciofi alla giudia* in all of Roma."

"Eat what?" she said, laughing.

"Artichokes, made in the style of Roman Jews."

Caroline made a face. "I don't like artichokes."

"You will like these," he said, with that absolute certitude she had once found so infuriating. "They are famous all over the world, not just in Trastevere." He paused, his eyebrows raised. "Well? What do you think?"

"I think it sounds like a perfect day. But—"

"Yes. I think so, too." Nicolo gathered her close and kissed her, his lips so soft, so sweet against hers that she feared her heart might stop beating. Then he smiled into her eyes and lowered her slowly to her feet. "Would you like to spend this day with me, Caroline?"

She hesitated. There was only one answer to give, and she gave it.

"Yes," she whispered. "I would love to."

THE PIAZZA NAVONA was incredible, with its three exquisite fountains all vying for attention.

"But I like the Fontana dei Fiumi best," Caroline admitted as they watched the water stream from the carved figures that represented the rivers of four continents.

"Of course," Nicolo said with a grin. "That's because it's the only one made by Bernini himself. The others were done by his students."

The Trevi Fountain was magnificent, too, although Nicolo was almost apologetic when he showed it to Caroline.

"It is big, and showy, and, perhaps, too large for the *piazza*," he said as they stood looking at its massive sculpted rocks and fanciful mythological figures. "But there is something very special about it, all the same."

"Who is that driving the chariot? The king of the sea? What was his name—Poseidon?"

"Only in Greece." Nicolo smiled. "He is Neptune to us here, in Italy. Do you know what they say about the Fontana di Trevi?"

Caroline nodded. "I think so. You're supposed to toss a coin into the water so—so you'll return to Rome someday."

"*Cara.*" His arm tightened around her. "Why do you suddenly tremble? Are you cold?"

I trembled because I'll never return to Rome, she thought, because when I leave tomorrow—and I will leave tomorrow—it will be forever.

"No. No, I'm fine." She gave him a quick smile. "Some of the spray splashed me, that's all. The water's chilly."

Nicolo let go of her and dug into his pockets. "Here."

She looked at the coins glinting against his palm, then at him. "Don't be silly," she said with nervous laugh. "It's just a myth."

"Of course. But a pleasant one, based on a custom that is rooted in history. In the old days, Romans tossed coins into fountains to placate the gods. Even the early Christians are said to have thrown coins onto Peter's tomb for good fortune."

Caroline smiled. "It must be universal. Back home, people toss coins into fountains for good luck, too."

"You see?" Nicolo pressed one of the coins into her hand. "Who are we to defy the gods? Go on, Caroline. You must turn your back, shut your eyes, and toss it over your shoulder.''

She hesitated a moment, and then she turned, and shut her eyes tightly, and wished for the impossible.

Please, she thought, oh, please, let Nicolo tell me he's fallen in love with me. I don't want to return to Rome—I never want to leave it. I want to stay here, with him, forever.

She spun around to watch the coin splash, but it was too late. It had vanished.

"Did my coin land in the fountain?" she asked.

Nicolo put his arm around her and drew her close.

"Of course. Did you make a wish, *cara*? Will you tell it to me?"

She felt the beginning sting of tears in her eyes, and she shook her head wildly, averting her face from him.

"If you tell someone what you wished, it won't come true." She forced a smile to her lips. "Didn't you say something about a picnic? My stomach's reminding me that all I've put in it so far today is coffee."

He grinned. "I almost forgot that insatiable appetite of yours," he said. "Come. We will go to the Campo de'Fiori, and you will tell me what you want for our lunch."

It was hard not to want everything at the vast open-air market. Luscious fruits and vegetables, sausages and cheeses of every description, breads that smelled as wonderful as they looked, lay heaped in profusion on market stalls shaded by cream-colored umbrellas.

"The Campo de'Fiori . . ." Caroline glanced at Nicolo as they strolled from vendor to vendor. "The Field of Flowers?"

"Yes." He smiled wryly. "Some would say that is a fanciful name for a place where heretics were put to the torch four centuries ago."

Her mouth dropped open. "Here?"

"Why do you look so surprised, *cara*? Wasn't it Salem, in your New England, where they drowned witches? Like many places, the good happened here as well as the bad." He gave an expressive shrug. "I think that is what I love most about my city. It's a place of reality, yes? To always smile, never to cry—it is a dream, but it is not the way life is."

His words made her throat tighten. No. But it didn't have to be that way, when you were in love. If only this day could last for the rest of her life. If only a miracle would occur...

"Caroline." Nicolo hugged her to him. "I have made you unhappy, telling you about the burnings," he said, dropping a kiss on her upturned face. "You have too soft a heart, *bellissima*. There is no sense in crying over what has been."

She wasn't, she wanted to tell him. She was crying for what would not be. But she only smiled and said he was right.

Nicolo bought a bit of this, a bit of that, until finally, when she was sure they had enough to feed a small army, he was satisfied.

"*Basta.* Now we will sit and have a coffee, yes? So you can enjoy the sights."

They sat at a rickety table on the perimeter of the square, under the shade of an umbrella, sipping *espresso*, eating anisette biscuits, and watching the large, colorful crowd.

Caroline was enthralled. "Does this go on every day?"

"Every morning, for who knows how many years. Roman housewives come here to buy the freshest fruit and vegetables. And flowers," he said, gesturing to an old woman carrying a woven basket. He handed her a bill, plucked a spray of violets from the basket, and presented it to Caroline with a flourish.

"Oh." She smiled as she buried her nose in the velvety petals. "They're lovely, Nicolo. Thank you."

"Nico," he said, very softly.

She looked up. He was watching her with such quiet intensity that, for just an instant, she felt as if there were no one else in the square but the two of them.

"Will you call me Nico, Caroline, as you did last night?" He reached for her hand and brought it to his lips. "There is something in the way you say it that makes my heart sing."

Her heart seemed to turn over. How was she ever going to leave him? Everything about him was so dear to her now; his smile, his face, the soft huskiness in his voice that told her he wanted her.

Perhaps she didn't have to leave him. What would she gain by running away? She would not stop loving him, just because she was in New York and he was here. And—and why was she being so precipitate? He had not yet said he loved her, but that didn't mean he never would. There was time for that. Plenty of time.

She was an adult, not a child, and there was no one to answer to back home. She was free to stay in Rome, not at the *palazzo*—she could never do that, never let Nicolo provide her with room and board and a salary, and yet take her into his bed each night. But she could find a job and a furnished apartment, and then she'd be free, free to give herself to Nicolo as his lover...

"What are you thinking, *cara*, that has brought such a glow to your eyes?"

Caroline looked at him. "Nothing," she said with a little laugh. "Just—just something I hadn't considered."

Smiling, he took her hand and drew her to her feet. "You can consider this something which is nothing in the car," he said. "We have a short drive ahead of us now.

They headed southeast from the city, the Ferrari moving as fast as the wind, following the "Via Tuscolana" signs for Frascati where, Nicolo insisted, they would find the best white wine in the world.

Caroline, who was feeling happier and happier, laughed at him teasingly.

"The absolute best?"

"Certainly." He smiled, too. "I am never wrong about such things."

She laughed, but he was only telling her the truth. He'd been right about the entire day: the fountains in Rome, the quiet beauty of the little villages they passed and the gentle sweep of the *campagna*. They bought the wine, then drove on, the time passing swiftly in a blur of easy laughter and pleasant conversation.

In midafternoon, they parked on the side of a dirt road and carried their picnic lunch to a grassy knoll that gave a perfect view of the dark blue waters of Lago Albano. Caroline discovered that Nicolo had not bought too much food, because they finished it all, right down to the last bit of crusty, delicious bread.

"Good?" he said, and she sighed with contentment.

"Wonderful."

He smiled as he lay his head in her lap. "Are you glad you came with me, *cara*?"

"Yes," she said softly. "Very glad."

"You aren't bored?"

"No. Of course not. Why would I be?"

He shrugged his shoulders. "It just occurred to me that you might have preferred to shop in the Via Veneto. Or the Piazza di Spagna. Cartier is there, and Bulgari..."

Caroline shook her head. "I've seen enough of places like that to last a lifetime. I'd much rather be here. It's beautiful."

"I'm glad. I have never brought anyone here before, and—"

"Not even Arianna?" Her lips clamped together and she stared at him in horror, unable to believe she'd really asked him such a question. "I'm sorry," she said quickly. "I didn't mean—"

"It's all right, Caroline." He sat up ad gave her a quick smile which she supposed was meant to be reassuring. But it wasn't; she could see that it was not a real smile at all. "The subject is not forbidden."

"Still, I didn't mean to pry." She looked down into her lap, plucked a blade of grass, and twisted it in her fingers. "It's just that—well, no one ever talks about her but—but she's always around, like a—a ghost or a shadow."

"There is no great mystery. I told you, she came to live with us after her parents were killed in an accident. A plane crash, somewhere in Argentina, I think."

"What was she like?"

"I have told you that, as well." There was tension now, in his face and in his voice. "She was young, she was very beautiful—"

"I don't mean what did she look like. I mean—I mean..." Caroline paused. "Anna confused me with her, remember? And—and the other night you—you said I was—"

"I remember what I said." He got to his feet and brushed off his pants. "I was wrong—and I was right."

"I don't understand what that means, Nicolo," Caroline said, as she rose and stood beside him.

He sighed. "It means, in some ways you are the same, and in others you are different."

"Can't you explain any better than that?" There was a sudden sharpness in her voice; she could hear it. She gave Nicolo a quick smile to soften it. "It's—it's weird to be compared to someone you've never seen."

He shrugged his shoulders. "She was a tease. She would smile at a man, lead him on a few steps, then turn cold." For the first time since Arianna's name had been mentioned, he smiled. "You are not like that, *cara*. I know that now."

"But—but in other ways, we're the same?"

Again, he gave that expressive shrug. "I thought, at first, you looked alike. But it's not so. She was not so fair, nor so tall—nor so beautiful. But there is a similarity just the same. Anna and I both saw it. A certain grace in the walk, a mystery in the smile..."

"Why did she go away?"

He stared at her for a long moment, and then he turned, stuffed his hands into his pants pockets, and stared out over the lake.

"I know I told you this, Caroline. She had no wish to settle down. She wanted to travel, to see the world—to have a career." His voice hardened. "In that, you and she are the same."

Caroline bit her lip to keep from telling him how wrong he was. Why would she want to travel any farther than his arms? This was where the world began and ended.

"And—she left you?"

There was a barely perceptible pause. "Yes."

She took a step toward him. But did you love her? She wanted to ask, but what was the point? Of course he'd loved her. She didn't want to hear him say it; it would only drive the pain she felt deeper into the heart.

Suddenly, he swung around and faced her. "I have no wish to talk of this any more."

Why would he? He had loved Arianna and she had run away from him, and now he was judging her by what Arianna had done. It wasn't fair, she thought angrily. She wasn't Arianna; she wasn't anything like her...

"Nico." She touched his shoulder and his muscles stiffened under her fingers. "Nico, it must have been—it must have been terrible for you, loving her and losing her. But—"

Nicolo shrugged. "It was an experience from which I learned something important."

Caroline hesitated. Instinct told her not to ask the question, but her heart demanded an answer.

"What?"

"That I chose unwisely." His eyes met hers, and she was stung by the cool practicality in those blue depths. "I made a mistake in asking a woman like Arianna to change her ways for me. Believe me, Caroline, it is not a mistake I will ever make again."

His words sent her heart plummeting.

"I can see that you'd feel that way," she said softly. "But—"

"Good." His tone was sharp, almost curt; he tried to soften it with a smile. "Then, we have nothing more to discuss. Come. We have dinner reservations at Romolo's, but first I must show you the sunset."

She stared at him. Then, slowly, she forced a smile to her lips.

"That sounds lovely."

By the time they'd stowed everything in the boot of the Ferrari and driven to a hilltop where, Nicolo said, they would have the best view, the sun was a fiery ball low on the hills. Caroline held her breath as they stood in the silence, watching as it began its final plunge, and, at just the moment it painted the world crimson, Nicolo put his hands on her shoulders.

"Caroline," he said softly. "I have something to ask you."

Her heart did a foolish leap, despite the conversation they'd had moments before. Perhaps the old gods had been listening, when she'd made her wish at the Trevi Fountain.

She felt her lips tremble as she smiled at him.

"What is it, Nicolo?"

"I have been thinking..."

"Yes?" Her heart was pounding harder and harder, as if it were getting ready to leap out of her breast.

He cleared his throat. "I know how you feel about these things, Caroline. You have told me often enough."

She stared at him, puzzled. "What things?"

"The things we discussed when I first brought you to the *palazzo*." He frowned. "And—the things we discussed the other night."

"I still don't—"

"Cristo!" His voice was harsh, edged with impatience. "Must I spell them out? You spoke of your feelings about men, about your career." He glared at her, as if it were her fault she couldn't remember. "Surely, you recall your own sentiments."

She did, in bits and pieces. She'd told him she didn't need a man in her life, that she had no wish for a home and family, that her career was all-important. But none of it was true—she'd only said it to cover her own growing confusion, a confusion she now realized had come out of what she'd begun to feel for him.

"Yes," she said, "I remember. But—"

"But still, you have a woman's needs. Yes. I told you that you did, even though you refused to admit it then." He smiled, and the lack of warmth in the smile chilled her. "I've given much thought to what you meant when you said those things—to what you really want, and—"

"What I meant? What I want? I don't understand, Nicolo."

"It is quite simple." The darkness was almost complete now; she could only see the faintest outline of his features, enough to know that they'd taken on a hard, determined cast. "You will stay in Roma."

Her breath caught. "Wait a minute. Let me tell you what I—"

"Not at the *palazzo*, of course." He frowned. "That would be difficult for us all. I will find you an apartment—something old and handsome, that you will like."

"Nicolo, please. I've thought about this, too, and—"

"And a studio."

She stared at him. "What?"

"Or a shop. Whichever you prefer. I don't know if there are places in Rome where you can study design. If there are, naturally I will pay for your courses."

Oh, God. God! He was asking her to be his mistress. This was what he'd wanted of her all the time; now, he was finally getting to it, baiting the trap not with jewels or furs but with what he assumed would matter to her.

"Otherwise, I will use my influence to find you an apprenticeship at one of the better fashion establishments." He smiled tightly. "Anna spends enough money at such places. Surely I can find one of them that would be willing to—"

"To—to help you along."

"Exactly."

Caroline took a deep breath. "Let me be sure I understand," she said softly. "You'll set me up in my own apartment—"

"Yes."

"Buy me a career—"

His jaw shot forward. "Why do you make it sound so—"

"So what? Cheap? Tawdry?" A smile trembled on her lips. "You're right, Nicolo. It won't be cheap at all. Just tally up the costs. An apartment. A studio. An apprenticeship. Oh, and I'll need spending money, too, of course. And clothes."

"Caroline. Listen to me—"

"No." She slapped his hands from her shoulders. "*You* listen. You can just forget it."

"What do you mean, forget it?"

"Can it. Stow it. Put it in your hat." She took a breath. "I mean no, I am not interested. That's not an American idiom. Don't pretend you don't understand it."

She swung away from him and started to the car. When she was halfway there, he caught up to her and spun her around to face him.

"You're being ridiculous! How can you say no to my proposal without even discussing it?"

"It's not a proposal," she said angrily. "It's—it's an attempt to buy me."

His fingers bit into her flesh. "I told you once, *cara*, I have never paid for a woman."

"It's a classier offer than the ones I'm accustomed to getting." Her head lifted sharply. "Hell, no one's ever offered me a career before."

"The career you long for, Caroline. Yes?"

"Yes," she lied, "that's right. I do long for it. But on my own terms, and by my own efforts." She threw out her hands. "You just don't understand—but then, why would you? You come from a world in which you make all the rules."

"Is that what you think?" He moved closer to her. Anger glittered coldly in his eyes. "You think I make the rules, eh? What of you? What rules do you make, *cara*? None that a sane man can comprehend."

"Just because you can't—"

"It is beyond me to understand why you would turn down what I offer when it's what you want." His arms swept around her rigid body. "You know you want me, Caroline. It does no good to pretend otherwise. I held you in my arms last night. I heard you cry out, I felt you tremble with need . . ."

"That was just sex," she said, the lie cold as winter ice on her tongue. "You were right about one thing, Prince Sabatini. I do have needs—and last night what I did was satisfy them."

In the last waning glow of daylight, she saw Nicolo's face tauten with fury as he teetered on the knife-edge of control. It took all her determination to stand her ground until finally he brushed past her.

"It's late," he snapped. "I have a long day ahead of me tomorrow. You will understand if I suggest we forget dinner and go straight home."

"And you'll understand if I leave Rome tomorrow morning." She stepped into the car and he slammed the door after her. "Just as soon as I can get a flight to New York."

"I will make the arrangements." He turned on the engine, slammed the car into gear, and shot her a sharklike smile. "I trust you'll have no objections if I use whatever influence I have with the airlines to get you the first available seat?"

Tears rose in Caroline's eyes and she turned her head blindly to the window.

"I'd be happy if you would."

Nicolo nodded. "Fine." His hands clamped down tightly on the steering wheel. "By this time tomorrow, your visit to Roma will be history. This is the correct idiom, Caroline, isn't it?"

"Yes," she whispered. She put her head back and closed her eyes. "Oh, yes, Your Highness, that's exactly the correct idiom."

It was the last either of them spoke as the Ferrari raced through the night.

CHAPTER TWELVE

ON A HOT summer afternoon a few weeks later, Caroline trooped wearily home from work and opened her mailbox to find a long white envelope bearing the logo of the Davis School of Design. She looked at it, then clasped it to her breast and closed her eyes.

"Please," she murmured as she climbed the steps to the fifth-floor Brooklyn Heights apartment she'd subleased for the summer, "please, let this be an acceptance!"

If it wasn't, she would just have to grit her teeth and start all over again.

Sighing, she unlocked the door, closed it after her and carefully relocked it again. She put the envelope down on the small table that served double duty as desk and dining surface, eased off her shoes, and stepped out of the cotton dress that felt as if it were stuck to her damp skin. She went into the tiny bedroom, stripped off her hose and slipped into a loose T-shirt and boxer shorts. Yes, she thought as she worked her hair into a French braid, that was better. Barefoot, she padded into her cramped kitchen and took a can of Coke from the refrigerator. Finally, she snatched up the envelope from the table where she'd left it and carried it to the one window that might, if she were lucky, catch a vagrant breeze from the river a block away.

She held the envelope to the light, squinting at it with one eye while she tried to read the first paragraph. Would it say, "Dear Miss Bishop, Thank you for your recent inquiry, but..." which was what the letters from Parsons and FIT had said. Or would it, by some miracle, say, "Yes, we approve of your credentials, yes, we have room for you in our summer classes, yes, yes, we want you..."?

"Oh, come on," Caroline muttered. "Just open the stupid thing and get it over with."

Still, she hesitated. What if Davis had denied her application, too? The practical part of her said it wouldn't be the end of the world. She wasn't broke—she'd found a job selling cosmetics at Macy's, just across the Brooklyn Bridge in Manhattan. It was a bit cheaper living here in an older neighborhood than in the heart of the city, so she hadn't had to tap into what she'd earned as companion to Anna Sabatini. She hadn't wanted to take the four months' pay from Nicolo, but he'd been coldly adamant.

"It was our agreement," he said, thrusting the check at her, and finally she'd swallowed her stupid pride and admitted to herself that he was right. That had been their agreement, and, if she was walking out on the deal earlier than expected, it was as much his fault as hers.

The money was sitting intact in the bank, earmarked for tuition at either the Fashion Institute of Technology or at Parsons for the autumn term, when at least one of the schools would admit her.

Caroline hitched her bottom onto the wide windowsill, put up one leg, and leaned back against the frame. It was just that September was too late. She wanted to get started now. Immediately.

"What's the rush?" a harried clerk had asked when Caroline had tried to talk her way into being permitted to enter a summer class that was already under way. "Surely it won't be the end of the world if you don't start school until fall."

Caroline had stared at her blankly before finally smiling faintly and agreeing that it would not be. She sighed, raised the can of Coke to her lips, and let some of the cool, sweet liquid ease down her throat. What would have happened, she wondered, if she'd told the woman the truth, that it just might be the end of the world, that she couldn't keep going through the days this way, with nothing to devote her energies to, nothing to occupy her thoughts—except Nicolo, and how much she despised him?

It amazed her that she'd ever believed herself in love with him, that she'd deluded herself into seeing his arrogance and his egotism as positive qualities. That she should have vasted time crying over him was not just amazing, it was ncredible. And that she couldn't stop thinking about him 10w was infuriating, never mind that the thoughts were an- ;ry ones and not the sloppy, sentimental stuff that had made 1er weep the first few nights after she'd left Rome.

She'd finally realized that what she needed was to com- nit mind, body and soul into something challenging and xciting. She grimaced as she took another swig of Coke. It eemed absolutely logical that that "something" should be 1er new career, but the schools had a different idea.

"Sorry, but we're booked," said the admissions officer at)ne.

"Classes have already started," said the clerk at the other.

And then, one Saturday, as she walked listlessly through Matisse exhibition at the Museum of Modern Art, Caro- ine had run into a girl she knew from catalog modeling.)ver ice tea and sandwiches, she'd mentioned her useless ittempts to gain last-minute admittance at design school.

"Yeah, I've heard it can be rough. How about DSD? Did ou try them?"

"I never even heard of DSD. What is it?"

The girl had grinned and taken a gulp of ice tea. "Very, ery small, and very, very choosy. They have some kind of ummer apprentice program—you know, they pay you a tipend and farm you out to some posh house like Given- hy or Calvin Klein."

Caroline had sighed. "I'd give my right arm for some- hing like that, but so would every other would-be designer 1 New York."

"Yeah, well, I'd give it a shot. From what I hear, they're ig on oddball backgrounds, not the usual, 'I've taken mpteen million courses' thing but the sort of stuff you've one. Modeling, a stint overseas, a few sketchbooks, maybe ome clothes you've made for yourself."

Caroline swung her leg to the floor, put down the Coke an, and with one determined yank, ripped open the enve-)pe.

"Dear Miss Bishop," she read aloud. "After a review of our credentials and your application, we are happy to of- :r you...."

"Yes!" she said joyously. "Yes!"

DSD not only wanted her; they wanted her enough to offer her six weeks working as an apprentice at Chanel, in Paris.

Beaming, Caroline scanned the rest of the letter. "If this is acceptable to you, please sign the enclosed forms, arrange for a current passport, and contact this office as soon as possible."

Caroline hugged herself as she danced to the telephone. Suddenly, life looked quite a bit brighter.

THE WOMAN she met with at DSD explained that Caroline had been very lucky. They'd almost had to turn her down because all their openings for the summer had already been filled.

"But then the young man who was slotted for this spot had to back out. Something about an incomplete grade on his college transcript."

Caroline tried to sound compassionate. "How unfortunate for him."

The woman nodded. "Yeah, but he's the nephew of one of our directors," she said with a just-between-us smile. "I bet he'll still get a spot for the summer if he gets things sorted out."

Caroline paled. "Are you telling me I might get bounced?"

"Oh, no, nothing like that." The woman became very businesslike. "Once you sign this contract, we're committed to you—and you to us."

Quickly, Caroline scrawled her signature on the proffered form. Nothing could stop her now. She was on her way to Paris, and to a new life...

At least, she thought she was—until the day before her flight, when a DSD representative phoned and told her there'd been a change of plan.

"Sorry about this, Miss Bishop," the man said briskly. "I'm afraid we've had to reassign you.

Caroline's face fell. "I'm not going to Paris?"

"No. But you're going some place just as good. In fact, I'm sure it will please you, considering the information on your résumé."

Milan, Caroline said to herself with that sudden, strange insight fate often provides. The floor seemed to give way beneath her. No, she thought, please, no, don't let it be Milan . . .

It wasn't Milan.

It was Rome.

THERE WAS NO WAY out of it. She had signed a contract and besides, why should she pass up six weeks' apprenticeship with a top-flight designer because she and Nicolo Sabatini would be living in the same city? Four million people lived in Rome. She wasn't going to run much risk of rounding a corner and coming face-to-face with him—and, even if she did, so what? When she'd been very little, not too long after her parents had died, she'd had bad dreams.

"Something awful's in the closet," she'd sobbed to Grams, and Grams had first held her and comforted her, then opened the door to show her that there was nothing inside but clothing.

"If you're scared of something, look it straight in the eye and it will go away," Grams had said.

And that was what she'd do now, if by some chance she bumped into Nicolo. Not that she was afraid of him; there was no reason she should be. Still, the principle was the same. The only way to banish the bogeyman was to look him in the eye without flinching.

And that was what she'd do if—*if*—she ever had the misfortune to run into Prince Nicolo Sabatini again.

But she didn't. The days passed quickly in hard, yet fulfilling work. Caroline was not only learning, she was doing what she'd wanted to do, channeling her energy into something positive.

But it wasn't helping. Instead of thinking of Nicolo less often, she was thinking of him more and more. The reason for it was obvious. Every narrow, cobble-stoned street, every white-pillared ruin, every little *ristorante*, reminded her of Nicolo and the time they'd spent together.

She hated herself for remembering, not just that last ugl
confrontation in the *campagna* but the things that had pre
ceded it, the good things, starting with the fun they'd ha
together and ending with that long, sweet night she'd spen
in his arms. But most of all she hated herself for awakenin
in the darkness night after night, with Nicolo's name on he
lips and tears on her cheeks.

She threw herself into her work harder than ever, doin
anything that was asked of her, from pinning hems t
sweeping the design-room floor to helping the showroon
models with their makeup, and all the while she counted th
days until she could leave this city and go back to New York
where she belonged. The only thing she ever refused to d
was to model.

But one morning, when she was only days from goin
home, two of the girls called in ill with summer colds. Ra
mondo, the designer, was frantic; an oil-rich sheikh wa
coming in for a private showing with his wives. There wa
no way to show the entire collection smoothly with tw
models missing.

"Caroline," he pleaded in his rich Italian *basso pro
fundo*, "you have modeled professionally, no? *Per favore*
you must help me just this once."

Her immediate inclination was to turn him down. But h
had been very kind to her the past few weeks, and she kne
he was right, that the showing would be a fiasco if it went o
this way.

She told herself she could manage this one last stint. I
wasn't catwalk modeling, it was a private showing; all sh
had to do was stroll through the small showroom, mount
carpeted platform faced with mirrors, look elegant and di
interested while the sheikh's wives made their selections.

"Caroline? Just this once, yes?"

She sighed. "All right."

Raimondo kissed her on both cheeks, then clapped h
hands and began barking out orders. Caroline fell easily int
the old, familiar routine. Out of her own clothing, into th
clothing marked off for her on the design board, a quic
check of hair and makeup, smile, toss back your shoulder
strut out from behind the curtain that separated the studi

from the private showroom and stride the length of it to the platform and turn, step, step, turn.

It wasn't as awful as she'd anticipated, partly because she greatly admired Raimondo's talent, partly because the audience was so small, just the sheikh, his wives, a handful of retainers, and a couple of the sheikh's Italian business associates brought along to translate—although one of the businessmen kept giving her glances that made her uncomfortable. She even thought he looked vaguely familiar, but then she realized it must be the type that seemed familiar. He was the sort of man she'd seen far too much of when she'd worked in Milan for International Models.

Afterward, Raimondo kissed her again.

"You see? That wasn't so difficult, was it?" he said, and, when Caroline admitted that it hadn't been, he said that in that case, would she please agree to do another private showing in midafternoon? The request had just come in.

Caroline sighed. She had survived this morning; how difficult would a repeat performance be?

But that afternoon, something made her hesitate just before she stepped out from behind the curtain. Her heart began to pound frantically, as if she were having an anxiety attack—but she wasn't prone to anything like anxiety attacks.

"Andiamo, andiamo," Raimondo whispered urgently.

Caroline nodded, drew a deep breath, made her entrance...

And came to a dead stop. Nicolo! Oh, God, he was here! He was in this room.

Raimondo's voice hissed again from behind the curtain. She stumbled forward, her legs leaden, afraid to let her eyes sweep the room, afraid not to. Maybe she was wrong. Maybe she was crazy. Maybe...

She was none of those things. Once she'd stepped onto the platform, there was nothing to do but turn, step, step, turn and nowhere to look but straight ahead.

The room swam around her. There he was, Prince Nicolo Sabatini, standing at the rear of the showroom, completely alone, his arms folded over his chest, watching her exactly as he had the first time she'd set eyes on him, with

such a fierce blend of desire and anger that her heart leaped
into her throat.

Look him in the eye, Caroline told herself. But Gram's
advice wasn't working. Looking Nicolo in the eye only made
her knees feel as if they were going to buckle. She glanced
away, but she knew Nicolo's gaze never left her. She had no
choice but to stand like a gazelle frozen by the cruel gaze of
the lion.

She was barely aware of the other models joining her on
the platform, followed by Raimondo himself, something he
did only for very important clients.

He cleared his throat delicately. "Would *il Principe* like
to see the gowns again?"

Nicolo stirred, leaned away from the wall, walked slowly
forward, his eyes never leaving Caroline.

"I wish to see that one," he said coldly, nodding at her.
"The others may leave."

The designer clapped his hands and the other girls exited
the room. Caroline wanted to go, too, but her feet felt
rooted to the platform.

Nicolo looked at the designer. "You may leave, as well."

"I, Your Highness?" Raimondo said, surprise coloring
his voice.

Nicolo waved his hands imperiously. "*Sì. Parte!* Get out
of here! How many times must I say it?"

It was the arrogant gesture and the insolent tone, that
freed her.

"How dare you order people around that way?" she said.

Raimondo turned white. "Caroline!" His eyes darted
from her to Nicolo and he babbled an apology, half in Ital
ian, half in English. "Signorina Bishop is not familiar with
our ways—"

"No. She is not." Nicolo's mouth twisted as he stopped
before the platform and looked up at her. "It is only her
own customs she respects."

"What—what would Your Highness like to know about
this gown? The fabric? The colors? Just tell me, Excel
lency, and—"

"That was your friend who was here this morning, wasn't it?" Caroline said. "I remember now—Antony, Antonio—"

"Antonini." Nicolo smiled coldly. "Yes. He remembered you, as well, from that night at the Sala dell'Arte. He thought he would do me a service by telling me that the Ice Princess who had caught my eye was right here, in Roma."

"Caroline. Your Highness." The designer wrung his hands. "Please. If there is a problem—"

"I don't know why you came here, Nicolo. We've nothing more to say to each other."

"We have a great deal to say. Get some clothing on. I will wait."

Caroline laughed incredulously. "Just listen to you." Her voice dropped to a cruel low. "'Get some clothing on,'" she mimicked. "'I will wait.'" She stepped forward, her hands on her hips. "You're damned right, you'll wait. You'll wait till hell freezes over, because I am not—"

"Would you prefer me to carry you to your dressing room, strip that gown from your body, and dress you myself?"

She stared at him, her face turning white with anger as she heard Raimondo's indrawn gasp. He would do it, too; she knew he would. After a moment, she spun on her heel and stalked across the platform to the door that led to the large communal dressing room.

The models, who were clustered at the door, stepped quickly out of her way.

"Caroline?" one whispered. "What's happening?"

"Something that should have happened weeks ago," she snapped. "Apparently, some men need to have things spelled out for them."

She pulled off the gown, kicked off the matching shoes, and dragged on the outfit she found most comfortable for working in the studio, a pair of worn denims and a baggy cotton T-shirt with "I Love New York" printed on it. She slapped a handful of cold cream on her face and tissued off the exaggerated makeup she'd worn for the showing, pulled her hair back into a ponytail, laced on her sneakers, and stalked back to the showroom where Raimondo was hovering over a glowering Nicolo.

"Signorina Bishop, *per favore*... If you would explain..."

"This has nothing to do with you," she said kindly. Her chin rose as she looked at Nicolo. "You could at least assure him of that," she snapped.

Nicolo's eyebrows lifted, but he nodded. "She is right, *signore*. I apologize for my temper and any inconvenience I have caused you, and I assure you that my grandmother will adore the things you showed me today. She will want to order everything."

"Everything?" the designer whispered.

Nicolo waved his hand. "Of course. I shall have her call you, yes?"

"Yes. Oh, certainly. Thank you, sir. Thank—"

"Basta!" Nicolo clasped Caroline's arm. Raimondo's words of gratitude faded as he hurried her out the showroom door to the street.

"Let go of me," she demanded as he hustled her toward his Ferrari, double parked, in the true Roman fashion, just outside the door. "Dammit, Nicolo, I said—"

"Get in the car."

"No!"

He opened the door and thrust her inside, then came quickly around and jumped in beside her.

"Nicolo. What the hell—"

The tires screamed as he jammed his foot to the floor and the car shot into traffic.

"So," he said through his teeth, "you never left Roma."

"Of course I did!"

"No wonder I couldn't locate you." The engine growled as he shifted into gear. "Cristo, when I think of the money I spent on detectives..." He threw her a cold look. "You would not believe how many Bishops there are in Manhattan, nor in Vermont and New Hampshire."

Caroline gaped at him. "Detectives. You hired detectives to find me? But—but why?"

His mouth thinned. "There is unfinished business between us," he said coldly.

She nodded. "Oh, I agree," she said, just as coldly. "There are things I should have said to you that I didn't. It will be a pleasure to get them off my chest!"

"I cannot believe you were here, in Roma, while I was employing half the detectives in New York to find you!"

"You should have hired one who'd heard of Brooklyn, because that's where I was."

"Brooklyn?" He glared at her. "But you said you were going home, to New York City."

"Brooklyn's a part of the city, but you wouldn't know that." She smiled sweetly. "It's like knowing the idioms, I guess. Unless you're American, you just can't understand certain things. Not that it matters—your detective wouldn't have found me anyway. I was subleasing an apartment, not renting in my own name."

The Ferrari swerved sharply as he pulled to the curb. He shut off the engine and swung toward her.

"So. All your talk of not being a model ever again was just that, eh? Talk—and nothing more."

Caroline crossed her arms over her breasts. "I don't see that that's any of your business."

"Do you work for International Models or another agency now?" She sat like stone, staring straight ahead. "What was the problem, *cara*? Did you miss the money? The excitement? Or was it the pleasure of having men's eyes on you that you could not do without?"

She spun and faced him. "For your information, Your Highness, today was the first time I've modeled since I left Rome."

"Really."

"Yes, really. I'm here as a design apprentice. It was only because they were short-handed that I agreed to help out and…" Their eyes met; she saw cool amusement in his gaze, and she flushed and swung away from his again. "I don't owe you any explanations."

"No?"

"No." She reached for the door handle. "Now, if you'll excuse me, it's time I—"

"I told you, Caroline, there is business between us."

"I can't imagine what."

"A few minutes ago, you agreed that there was."

Caroline eyed him coldly. "Only because I realized I never did get around to telling you that you are, without questions, the most insolent, willful, egocentric human being I've ever met!"

Nicolo laughed. "What a charming list of adjectives, *cara*. I'm impressed."

"Don't be. And don't call me 'cara,' dammit!"

"Don't be vulgar."

"I'll be as vulgar as I like. You don't own me, Your Highness. I am my own woman, and—"

He caught her face in his hands. "You are my woman," he growled, and before she could say another word, he kissed her.

Her hands came up and clamped onto his wrists. "Don't," she said.

But he ignored her, his mouth moving slowly over hers, not with anger, not even with desire, but with something so sweet, so dear, that Caroline began to tremble.

Her fingers curled around his wrists. "Don't," she said again, but the word was a lie, a whisper without meaning. Her lips parted under his, she moaned softly, and all at once she knew that she had never, not for a heartbeat, stopped loving him. How could she have? He was part of her; she was part of him. She would love him forever, despite everything he was.

Her eyes opened slowly as he drew back. His eyes swept over her face, and he smiled.

"Carissima," he whispered.

Caroline swallowed. "This—this won't solve anything. It won't prove anything."

He let go of her and slipped out from behind the wheel of the car. She waited while he came around to her side and opened the door.

"Come with me," he said, holding out his hand.

Like a sleepwalker, she put her hand into his, stepped onto the pavement, let him lead her forward . . .

"Wait a minute," she said. She dug in her heels and came to a grinding halt. "Wait a damned minute—"

Nicolo turned and took her in his arms. "I have told you repeatedly," he said. "It is unladylike for such words to come from such a beautiful mouth."

"I'll say whatever I damned well please!"

His mouth closed on hers. He kissed her deeply, until she was clinging to his shoulders, and then he drew back.

"And I will silence you when you do, *cara*." He smiled just a little. "We will see which of us lasts the longer. Now, come with me. We were going to settle our differences, once and for all."

"Nicolo! Are you crazy? Where are you taking me?" she demanded as he tugged her after him.

"We are in the Forum Boarium. Do you see that church ahead? It is Santa Maria in Cosmedin, and it is very old."

Wild laughter bubbled in Caroline's throat. "You've already taken me on a tour of Rome. I don't want another one!"

"What you are getting is not a tour, but a chance to tell the truth, Caroline."

She stumbled after him the length of the church portico, bumping against him when he came to a sudden stop.

"All right." She looked at him. His voice had taken on a strange, almost solemn tone. "We are here."

"Where?"

"Here," Nicolo said, nodding at the wall before them.

Caroline looked from him to the wall. A large, round stone plaque was set into it, depicting the face of a human or, perhaps, a god. She could see that it was very old—and somehow very frightening. It had two small, dark holes for eyes, a straight nose, and an open mouth that was a slash of darkness.

A tremor danced along her skin. "What is that?" she whispered.

Nicolo put his arm around her waist. *"La Bocca di Verità,"* he said. "The Mouth of Truth."

Caroline stared at the face. It was on the wall of a Christian church, but there was no doubt in her mind that the sculpture was pagan. It looked dangerous and alien, and suddenly she wanted to get as far from it as she could.

"Why does it look so—so—"

"In ancient times, my ancestors believed that if you told a lie while putting your hand into the mouth, it would bite off the hand."

"I don't like it," she said positively.

Nicolo's mouth twisted. "One does not like or dislike the Mouth of Truth, Caroline."

"No? Well, maybe Romans take that approach. But I'm an American, I don't like it, and I'm leaving."

His arm held her fast. "All you have to do is answer one question."

"I am not in the mood to play games," she said with false bravado. "If this is your idea of fun—"

"Put your hand in the mouth, *cara*."

She looked at him as if he were mad. "Don't be ridiculous!"

Nicolo took her hand and forced it toward the dark, slashing opening.

"Put your hand in," he insisted. "Then look me in the eye, and answer my question."

His grasp on her hand was fierce; there was no way she could free herself. But what was there to be afraid of? The mouth was frightening to look at, but it was harmless.

"All right," she said angrily. "Let go. I'll do it myself." She took a deep breath, and jabbed her fingers into the gaping mouth. Nothing happened—not that she'd really thought anything would—although there was a nervous tingle in her fingers. "Well? What happens next?"

"Now you answer the question."

"Honestly, Nicolo, this is—"

"The question, Caroline. Are you prepared to answer it?"

Their eyes met, and all at once it seemed hard to breathe. She swallowed dryly, then nodded.

"Yes, I'll answer your question. What is it?"

He lifted his hand and laid it against her cheek, his fingers cool and firm against her skin.

"It's a very simple one, *cara*," he said quietly. "Do you love me?"

Caroline jerked her hand back, and Nicolo caught it and held it in his.

"You must tell the truth," he said. "Or face the wrath of the gods."

She laughed nervously. "This is crazy! I don't believe in such nonsense."

Nicolo shrugged. "Nonsense? I'm not so sure, *cara*. That day at the Fontana di Trevi, you threw in a coin as all tourists do, so that you would some day return to Rome. And here you are."

"Well, yes, but—"

"As for me, I wished that I would not lose you." He smiled. "And here you are, back in my arms."

His words went straight to her heart, and she remembered the private wish she'd made that day, that Nicolo would tell her he loved her.

She smiled tremulously. "Is that—is that really what you wished?"

"You must answer my question first," he said, his eyes on hers. "Do you love me, Caroline?"

She stared at him. Such a simple question—and yet, such a dangerous one. To tell him the truth would be to reveal her inner self, she would leave herself exposed and vulnerable and—

He brought her hand to his lips.

"Will it help you if I tell you first that I love you," he whispered, "that I adore you with all my heart?"

Her breath caught, trembled in the air between them. These were the words she had longed to hear, the ones she had wished for that day at the Trevi Fountain.

"Caroline?" He smiled. "Have you nothing to say to me, *cara*?"

"I—I won't be your mistress," she whispered. "No matter what you say."

His brow furrowed. "My mistress? *Santa Maria*, what sort of man do you think I am? I love you, Caroline. That means I want to marry you, to make you my wife."

"Your wife?" She laughed, even though tears were glistening in her eyes. "Oh, Nico..."

"You have yet to answer my question," he said sternly. "Do you love me?"

"Yes," she said, "of course I do. I love you with all my heart."

Nicolo closed his eyes, then opened them again. "I knew it! But when you said what you did about the night we'd spent together..."

"It was a lie," Caroline whispered. She leaned closer to him and lay her head against his shoulder. "I wanted to hurt you, Nico. You'd hurt me so badly—there I was, head over heels in love with you, and you were asking me to be your mistress."

"I was asking you to be whatever you wished to be, *cara*." His jaw tightened. "It was stupid, and I suppose I did a bad job of it, but it was not easy, offering to set aside my rigid Old-World principles and give you the freedom you wanted."

"Oh, you aren't rigid at all! I want to be an old-fashioned wife to you, Nicolo."

"Are you sure?" He cupped her face and looked deep into her eyes. "I made a mistake with Arianna. I tried to change her, to make her into a woman she could not be." He gathered Caroline into his arms and held her in a close, almost fierce embrace. "I will not make such a mistake again!"

"Nico," Caroline whispered, "listen to me. I want you. Only you, do you understand? I want to make you a home, to bear your children..."

He silenced her with a kiss. When it ended, she looped her arms around his neck and asked the one question that had yet to be answered.

"Are you sure it's me you want," she murmured, "and—and not Arianna?"

Nicolo smiled. "Arianna and I were wrong for each other in dozens of ways. I realized that almost the instant she left me."

"Yes, but perhaps someday, if she comes back..."

"She has always come back—she loves Anna very much. It's just that no one ever knows when." He smiled. "I suspect you will like her, *cara*, when you meet."

"Well," Caroline said thoughtfully, "maybe. I mean, the next time she shows up—"

"You can tell me what you think of her tonight, when we all have dinner at the *palazzo* and tell Anna our news."

Caroline stared at him. "You mean, Arianna's here?"

"*Sì.* She has been for weeks."

"And—and she's still single?"

Nicolo laughed softly. "What will it take to convince you, *cara*? Yes. She is here, she is unmarried, she is still very lovely—but I don't love her. I love you."

Caroline cocked her head. "Put your hand in the Mouth of Truth," she said, "and I might just believe you."

"You American women," he said, "you ask too much of a man!" He turned and put his hand into the stone mouth. "*Ti amo, mi Carolina,*" he said softly, his eyes on hers. "I will love you for all eternity. I swear it, by all the gods."

Caroline smiled as Nicolo's arms closed around her.

The gods of the Caesars had done themselves proud.

ROME—'the Eternal City'

Everywhere you go in Rome, you feel history all around you: not just in the imposing, world-famous monuments, but also in every quiet street, where a picturesque court-yard, festooned with washing and crowded with colorful plants, may have a two-thousand-year-old column built into its walls, or a beautiful medieval fountain. It's this casual blend of old and new that makes the city so fascinating—it's full of secret corners for you to discover...

THE ROMANTIC PAST

The ancient Romans—so they claimed!—were descended from the gods. They were first brought to Italy by the Tro-jan warrior **Aeneas**, son of **Venus**, goddess of love, and Rome itself was founded by **Romulus** and **Remus**...the sons of the god **Mars**. Their mother was a **Vestal Virgin** who was condemned to death for breaking her vow of chastity—her twin babies were abandoned, to die, but, so the legend goes, were suckled by a **she-wolf**—now the emblem of the city.

Rome's full of such colorful legends, but here's one you can try out for yourselves, if you visit *la Bocca di Verità*—the Mouth of Truth—an ancient sculpture in the form of an eerie, openmouthed face. Its origins are lost in the mists of time, but legend has it that, if you put your hand into the mouth and tell a lie, it will bite your fingers off! Once an unfaithful wife, suspecting that her jealous husband was going to test her fidelity in this way, arranged to have her lover standing by. When the time came to put her hand in the mouth and swear that she'd never been untrue, she pretended to feel faint. The lover generously offered to help support her while she made her vow. With her husband's arm around her waist and her lover's around her shoulders, she put her hand fearlessly in the gaping hole and swore that she'd never let any other man touch her...except of course, this kind stranger who was being so helpful!

THE ROMANTIC PRESENT—pastimes for lovers...

Rome has some of the most famous sights in the world—the **Colosseum**, the **Pantheon**, **Vatican City**...it's impossible to do justice to them all! But there's so much to see and do that, wherever you wander in the city, you really can't go wrong!

For a magnificent view of Rome spread out below you, you can't do better than climb the steep stone steps from the busy **Piazza Venezia** to the top of the **Capitoline Hill**—Rome's still run from here, as it has been for thousands of years. You can look straight down into the **Forum**, the heart of ancient Rome, with its many temples, and across to the **Palatine Hill**, where the Roman Emperors had their splendid palaces, and lived out their scandalous lives!

While you're here, there's the **Capitoline Museum**—well worth a visit—and the sinister cliffs of the **Tarpaean Rock**. Roman traitors were cruelly flung to their deaths from here...

From this quiet corner you can plunge—hopefully a little less precipitously!—into the bustling modern city. You're not too far from the stylish and expensive shops around the **Piazza di Spagna**; the prices may be beyond your pocket, but at least you can window-shop—and dream! The beautiful piazza itself, with its famous **Spanish Steps**, was once the heart of Rome's artistic colony—you're walking in the footsteps of the English Romantic poets **Keats** and **Shelley**.

Now it's a meeting place for young people from all over the world . . . and you're bound to make friends here!

If you need a break from the fast-paced street life of the city, you're never far from a tranquil park. Just a stone's throw from the Piazza di Spagna are the elegant **Villa Borghese Gardens**—you can stroll for hours by its beautiful lakes, exploring secluded valleys and tiny mock temples.

On the other side of the city is the less well known **Villa Celimontana Park**. It's perched on the **Caelian Hill**, so when you've visited the Colosseum and Forum it's perfectly placed for a quiet picnic. This is where many Roman lovers come to wander hand in hand, so the air is full of romance . . .

When it's time for dinner, you'll be spoiled for choice. A warning about Italian food: if you're on a diet, stay away! The dishes are among the most delicious—and fattening—in the world. Try *antipasto misto*—mixed hors d'oeuvres, all delicious, heaped on your plate. For your main course, a Roman specialty is *saltimbocca* . . . literally, "jump in your mouth." It's tender veal rolled around delicately seasoned ham and cooked in wine. Another culinary highlight is *carciofi alla giudia*—mouthwatering artichokes. If you still have room for dessert, it's got to be *tiramisu*, a delectable coffee-flavored trifle.

The wine that inevitably accompanies your meal will be just as delicious, and may well come from one of the small towns near Rome—perhaps the famous **Frascati** or **Orvieto**.

Many of the most romantic restaurants are in **Trastevere**—Rome's Bohemian quarter, across the **River Tiber** from the center of the city. It's always worth a visit, particularly at the end of July, when the *Festa dei Noantri* is held, a traditional extravaganza of music, dancing and celebration.

Another highlight of the year is the summer season of opera spectacularly performed in the enormous ruins of the **Baths of Caracalla**. There could be no better setting for the splendor of grand opera, nor for the huge talents of its singers **Pavarotti, Domingo** and **Carreras**—this is where the once-in-a-lifetime concert of the "three tenors" was performed in 1990. Let's hope you see something as memorable!

DID YOU KNOW THAT...?

★ the **Vatican City** is an independent state within Rome, with its own administration, including its own stamps and postal service. Post your postcards in St. Peter's Square!

★ anyone can apply for a public audience with the **Pope**.

★ many of Rome's attractions are **underground**: there's a whole network of eerie catacombs, underground churches, secret caves and hidden rivers...

★ the Italian currency is the **lira**.

★ the looks and signs of love are universal, but in Italian "I love you" is *"Ti amo"*.

POSTCARDS FROM EUROPE

HARLEQUIN PRESENTS®

Travel across Europe in 1994 with Harlequin Presents. Collect a new Postcards from Europe title each month!

Don't miss
YESTERDAY'S AFFAIR
by Sally Wentworth
Harlequin Presents #1668

Available in July wherever Harlequin Presents books are sold.

HPPFE7

Hi!
I arrived safely in England and have found Nick. My feelings for him are as strong as ever, but he seems convinced that what we once shared belongs in the past. My heart won't accept that.
Love, Olivia

Fifty red-blooded, white-hot, true-blue hunks
from every State in the Union!

Look for MEN MADE IN AMERICA! Written by some of
our most popular authors, these stories feature fifty of
the strongest, sexiest men, each from a different state in
the union!

Two titles available every other month at your favorite
retail outlet.

In May, look for:

KISS YESTERDAY GOODBYE by Leigh Michaels (Iowa)
A TIME TO KEEP by Curtiss Ann Matlock (Kansas)

In June, look for:

ONE PALE, FAWN GLOVE by Linda Shaw (Kentucky)
BAYOU MIDNIGHT by Emilie Richards (Louisiana)

You won't be able to resist MEN MADE IN AMERICA!

Travel across Europe in 1994
with Harlequin Presents and...

As you travel across Europe in 1994, visiting your favorite countries with your favorite authors, don't forget to collect four proofs of purchase to redeem for an appealing photo album. This photo album can hold over fifty 4" × 6" pictures of your travels and will be a precious keepsake in the years to come!

One proof of purchase can be found in the back pages of each POSTCARDS FROM EUROPE title...one every month until December 1994.

To receive your gift, please fill out the information below and mail four (4) original proof-of-purchase coupons from any Harlequin Presents POSTCARDS FROM EUROPE title plus $3.00 for postage and handling (check or money order—do not send cash), payable to Harlequin Books, to: IN THE U.S.: P.O. Box 9048, Buffalo, NY, 14269-9048; IN CANADA: P.O. Box 623, Fort Erie, Ontario, L2A 5X3.

Requests must be received by January 31, 1995.
Please allow 4–6 weeks after receipt of order for delivery.

Name: _____
Address: _____
_____
_____
City: _____
State/Province: _____
Zip/Postal Code: _____
Account No: _____
ONE PROOF OF PURCHASE

077 KBY